No More
PRETENDING

Bette Hawkins

BELLA
B O O K S

2017

Bella Books, Inc.
P.O. Box 10543
Tallahassee, FL 32302

Printed in the United States of America on acid-free paper.

First Bella Books Edition 2017

Editor: Lauren Humphries-Brooks
Cover Designer: Linda Callaghan

ISBN: 978-1-59493-544-2

About the Author

Bette Hawkins hails from Melbourne, Australia. She lives with her long-term girlfriend and their very spoiled dog. In addition to writing, Bette's favorite pastimes include playing the electric guitar, watching films, cooking and reading.

Acknowledgments

Thanks to my girlfriend, for her support and encouragement. And for not minding when I disappear into my laptop for hours on end.

Dedication

To Suzie-Q

CHAPTER ONE

Lauren Langham stepped out of the car, lifting her sunglasses from her eyes. She pushed them back into her hair and looked around at the neighboring homes near the cottage. People had warned her that the town was small and very different from what she was used to. As she passed through the streets, she had noticed children playing on the sidewalks and strangers waving hello. The lawns were green and well kept, the houses all looked freshly painted, and there were no buildings taller than two stories high. It was the very definition of quaint. This town made New York City seem like an ant farm, considering the way people rushed around there, their eyes settling on nobody.

The new environment was a relief to her. Lauren had been craving peace, and she could already see that she would be able to find it here. Although her job had brought her to town, she hoped that there would be time for relaxation as well. She didn't even need to be in town this early, but she had wanted an extra few weeks to unwind and settle in.

Texas Twist was her third collaboration with director Sal Black. The leading man was Josh Lawson, with whom she had also worked in the past. When she read the script, she'd rolled her eyes at how corny it was. Pressure from her agent, who always wanted her to take roles like this, helped her to overcome her reservations. The promise of a large payday helped too. Although she had never been a very money-oriented person, she had made some unwise decisions lately and this would help her to recover from them.

Lauren looked approvingly at the cottage. Her assistant Melinda had rented it for her so that she would have complete privacy for the next three months. It was as lovely as it had looked in the pictures, white with green shutters, a large front porch and, she knew, a big backyard. When she was a kid, she had stayed briefly in a house with the same color scheme. The house had represented stability, her great-aunt exposing her to discipline and warmth in equal parts. She had spent long happy days exploring every clean corner of that house before she'd been yanked away again by her folks. Smiling, Lauren realized that she had forgotten all about her childhood wish for a house with green shutters until this moment.

She intended to make her daily life for the next few months as simple as it could be. The plan was that she would devote herself to work and then come home to cook, read and sleep. A period of hard work balanced with some rest would do her good.

Chester, her beloved dog, was waiting patiently on the passenger seat. It was important to her that she had been able to bring him along, given that right now he was the most constant presence in her life. When she walked around to unclip him from the seat belt, he jumped excitedly toward her and she gathered him up in her arms.

"This is our new house, boy. Do you like it?"

When she entered the cottage, she was even more impressed by it. It was beautifully furnished with antiques settled comfortably on plush carpets. The owners had decorated the walls with framed pictures, and there was lots of natural light.

The house had such a great energy that she was certain she was going to be happy here.

As she walked around, she was struck by the feeling of being completely alone for once. After years of the full movie star treatment and all the coddling that came with it, she worried sometimes that she had lost the ability to do things for herself. There was always someone else to make decisions and solve problems. At first, as a fiercely independent young actor, she had resisted the help, but she had long since given up on that. Lauren wanted to get closer to the person she had been before all of this. As a first step, Lauren had asked her assistant to stay in New York and work for her remotely. Melinda could be a lifesaver, but a break would be healthy for her. At the very least, Lauren could do her own grocery shopping.

A couple of her friends had teased her about her new goals. They had pointed out the ridiculousness of her trying to give away the Hollywood lifestyle while she was working on a mainstream film. The six-figure sum she was getting paid made her especially guilty, because it wasn't a role that she could feel proud of. Lauren had not tried to explain much to anyone. There was no point when she couldn't tell anyone the real reason for her resolutions.

When she was finished unpacking her suitcases, Lauren decided to take a walk and explore the town. It was the sort of place where you could walk from one edge to another without any need for a car. She assumed that most of her co-stars and the crew would be flying out on the weekends to nearby cities, rather than spending all of their time here. It was what she would have done herself six months ago.

Soon she came to the main strip of stores. There was a grocery store, a dry cleaner, a butcher, and a couple of other small stores. A diner stood in the middle of the row, with a simple red sign that said *Joe's*. She looked over the menu posted in the window before she went in. There was nothing fancy listed on it, just good simple food.

Lauren walked across the checked floor and slid into a booth. The red vinyl crinkled against her back. She tried to act like she didn't notice as the few other patrons in the diner looked over at her. Lauren averted her eyes to the table then self-consciously glanced up again. An older man gave her a friendly wave before looking back to his newspaper. She smiled to herself.

Lauren scanned the specials on the board behind the counter. She had missed breakfast and everything looked delicious. It took a few moments for her to realize that the waitress was talking to her. Lauren's glance shifted over in order to greet her...and Lauren froze.

The woman was beautiful, with shoulder-length red hair, pale skin, and warm brown eyes. In fact, she was so striking that Lauren was tongue-tied.

"Do you need another minute?" The waitress smiled uncertainly, her full lips parting. It was a stunning smile.

Lauren had no idea how long she had been sitting there just staring. Judging by the way the waitress was looking at her now, she gathered that it had been for an uncomfortable length of time.

"No, thank you. Can I have the chicken-fried steak please?" Lauren said quickly. She forced her voice to sound clear and confident. For years she had been getting by on strategies like that. Acting had helped a lot with her shyness.

Lauren cleared her throat and fixed her gaze over the woman's shoulder to avoid looking at her face again. She was supposed to be focusing on herself and not turning her head for the first pretty face she saw. Her eyes drifted to the name tag clipped to the front of the waitress's uniform: *Harper*, a name that would be suited to a character in a play or a movie about a Southern lady. The name sounded musical, just like the woman's voice. Then Lauren realized with horror that she was accidentally staring at the woman's chest, and looked away.

"Sure, coming right up." Harper said it sweetly but Lauren caught the question in her tone.

Lauren watched her walk away. Her soft aqua uniform complemented the flaming red hair. Like everything else in here, the uniform belonged to the 1950s. It looked incredible on her. The retro style fit Harper perfectly, because her face was timeless. She looked like she would be at home no matter what decade she lived in. Harper had the kind of figure that Lauren's colleagues hired personal trainers and chefs and even plastic surgeons to try to create. Yet Harper looked at ease with her beauty in a way that gave the impression that it came to her naturally.

It wasn't like Lauren to react to a woman like this, for her to be so instantly attracted. Thanks to her job, she met stunning women every day of her life. She had walked red carpets with women that society decided were the most beautiful people in the world. Most of them just didn't interest her in that way. Looks had never been that important to her, partly because she knew how much of an illusion they often were. A beautiful woman could be as dull or mean as anyone else. When she dreamed about being in a long-term relationship, her fantasies centered on being with someone that she could really talk to.

Lauren berated herself for the way she was thinking and how quickly she had noticed Harper. So much for wanting to spend some time on her own. As soon as she told herself that she couldn't have something, she wanted it more than ever. The fact that she was checking out a stranger so quickly after arriving in town only reinforced how important it was for her to stay focused on work. There was nothing wrong with feeling a blast of desire, but she didn't have to act on it or even think about trying to act on it. There was no reason to think that Harper had any interest in her, which only made the whole thing more stupid.

Lauren pulled her script from her handbag. She had work to do.

CHAPTER TWO

"One chicken-fried steak," Harper called out to the cook. Jimmy gave her a thumbs-up.

Harper took the coffeepot from its warmer and approached the customer again. She wondered where she'd seen this woman before. Usually she had a good memory for names and faces, but she couldn't place where or how they'd met. The woman had papers laid out in front of her now, occasionally scribbling in the margins. Harper walked slowly toward her.

"You new in town?" Harper asked. There was no way that the woman was local. Harper knew everyone who lived here by name, especially everyone close to her age. Harper guessed that the connection might be from school in New York. It would be an odd coincidence to run into an old classmate here, but stranger things had happened. The woman looked up; she had very green eyes. She was quite pretty actually, with well-defined cheekbones and thick dark eyebrows.

"Yes," the woman said sharply, adding nothing.

For a moment, Harper forgot which question she had asked. The customer pointedly looked away and trained her eyes on the page in front of her. Harper raised her eyebrows, then leaned over and filled the woman's coffee cup in silence. It was hard to understand why such a simple question would cause a reaction like that, but some people were just rude.

Harper moved to wipe down a nearby table. She looked around for Sue to share her annoyance, but Sue was probably on a cigarette break. Harper heard Jimmy call the order, and she headed toward the counter to pick it up. She wasn't looking forward to going back to the ice queen's table, although of course she would remain polite and professional. Harper paused when she felt Sue's hand on her arm. Sue was still breathless after running in from outside.

"Why didn't you tell me she was here?" Sue asked.

"Tell you who was here?" Harper replied. "Should I know what you're talking about?"

"That's Lauren Langham." Sue waited for the penny to drop then rolled her eyes. "You really don't know? How have you missed this? They're shooting a movie here and she's one of the stars. She's a little early though, I thought they weren't starting till next month."

Harper finally nodded. There had been a lot of background chatter about the movie, but she hadn't paid much attention to it. It sounded like a romantic comedy from what she heard, so not really her kind of thing. Once upon a time she'd kept up with pop culture, but she had other things on her mind these days.

"I guess this is proof you don't listen to anything I say," Sue joked. "And haven't you seen a movie in the last five years? How can you not know who she is?"

Harper shrugged helplessly. "I just don't?"

The two of them stared at Lauren, who was obliviously looking down. Harper suddenly realized where she knew Lauren. She'd been in a movie Harper had seen years ago, in New York—a film that had made a big impression on her at the time. It was a shame that Lauren was disappointing in real life. Harper supposed that actors like her had so much money and attention thrown at them that they forgot what the real world was like.

"Do you mind if I take over the table?" Sue asked eagerly. "I'm not trying to steal your tip; you can have it. She always seems like such a sweetheart in her movies, I bet she's got a big heart."

"I doubt it, but I'll split it with you whichever way she goes. Fifty-fifty. You'd better get that over there before it gets cold," Harper said. She didn't really care to deal with a Hollywood diva anyway. There was nothing more boring to her.

"Thanks, you're a doll," Sue said, taking the plate from her and heading over toward the table.

Lauren looked up from her script as an older waitress with a friendly, open face came toward her. Lauren's eyes flicked back over to Harper, whom she could see behind the counter, leaning forward on her elbows, laughing and joking around with the cook. That smile lit up her whole face. Lauren could see her profile, her long limbs folded easily in front of her.

Lauren had really hoped to have the chance to speak with Harper again. She was aware that she had acted strangely by not answering Harper's question and she wanted to rectify the mistake she had made. When Harper had tried to strike up a conversation, she hadn't known how to talk about why she was here without sounding like she was bragging about being an actor. It was nice to speak with someone who didn't know who she was, and she hadn't made the most of it. Lauren was used to seeing the dawning of recognition on a person's face right before they started treating her differently.

The second waitress, whose badge read *Sue*, leaned over to refill her coffee cup. "Is there anything else you need?"

"No, thanks."

"I think it's wonderful that you're here, Miss Langham. I hope you'll come back and see us again."

"I'm sure I will."

Now and then Lauren would watch Harper while she went about her business, but there was no opportunity to interact with her again. Feeling disappointed, Lauren got up to leave.

"How was everything?" Sue asked her as she passed.

"Very good thank you," Lauren said. "Best meal I've had in a while."

Sue smiled at her broadly, and Lauren started to leave the café with one last backward glance toward Harper. Harper was standing at someone else's table now and chatting comfortably with them. Lauren paused and allowed herself to take just one last glance, to admire the way Harper looked when she laughed.

Harper must have felt Lauren's eyes on her because she looked up at just that moment. The laugh died on her lips. They held eye contact for a moment, Lauren feeling lost in her warm brown-eyed gaze. Harper broke the stare first and returned to her conversation.

Lauren turned quickly and walked away.

"I was right, she has a *huge* heart," Sue said gleefully, using her tongue to wet her thumb and then peeling off a note to give to Harper.

"Thanks. Pity she has such a chip on her shoulder to go with it," Harper said, pocketing the money. Lauren had looked at her with such an odd expression on her face just now. Harper couldn't believe that a person could get so bent out of shape at not being recognized.

"Oh, she's just a little shy I think. I can't wait 'til Josh Lawson comes in here. I bet his...tip will be enormous." Sue gave an exaggerated wink and Harper laughed at her corny joke.

Harper didn't know how she would survive in this job without Sue, who had become one of her closest friends since they started working together. Spending so much time with her was a distraction from the fact that this was not where Harper was supposed to be. There was nothing wrong with being a waitress, and being one here in particular was a good job, but she had been thrown off her path. Once she had been ambitious, with big goals. But since her mother's illness, she'd had to leave her job at her uncle Stephen's law firm in New York to look after her father and brother. It was supposed to be a short break, just until things settled down. That was two years ago.

When her mother died, the world stood still for her and yet, inexplicably, it kept moving for everyone else. It was difficult for her to wrap her mind around how she was supposed to go on. At first, it was all about just trying to get through the days. Then it became clear that her father and brother just couldn't take care of themselves.

She never imagined that working at Joe's would be anything other than temporary, but the days stretched out into a couple of lonely years, taken up with care for her brother and her dad, who had started drinking too much. A lot of her friends from high school moved away a long time ago and she had little in common with the ones who stayed. In truth, she had always been an outsider here, and once upon a time she couldn't wait to get away.

The experience of seeing that movie that starred Lauren Langham belonged to a different life. Harper most likely saw it in an art house theater in the East Village, and had probably gone out with friends afterward for a drink. She had been such a different person back then. Life was a funny thing, the way a little piece of your past could come back to you in the strangest ways.

Over the next couple of days, Lauren would walk back into her mind. Harper thought that perhaps the connection that she'd made to her past had made her reflective. Although she liked to think that she didn't care about the movie getting made in their town, she had to admit that there was something a little bit exciting about it.

Maybe there was even something a little bit exciting about *her*. The actress might not be the nicest person around but she was a stranger, and there were precious few of those in this town.

CHAPTER THREE

For the next couple of weeks, Lauren spent most of her time in the cottage, relaxing and procrastinating about work. It was easy to be lazy in this town. It was hot and the pace was slow. Nobody was in a rush to do anything. Sweat made her clothes stick to her skin, so she passed the hours lying around in the air-conditioning or out on the porch, letting the breeze cool her down. She drank homemade iced tea and chewed on ice chips.

Lauren had brought a handful of films set in the South with her because she'd planned on studying them to work on her character's accent. It wasn't a difficult one to pull off, and she knew that she could get it right without the help of a coach. At least, she could if only she could motivate herself to spend some time on it. The movies lay unwatched on her coffee table while she read books that had nothing to do with work. Whenever she picked up the script to start learning her lines, she just wound up putting it right back down again.

For the thousandth time lately, she was entertaining the idea of quitting the whole business. The thought of it always made her excited and terrified at the same time. What kind of person would she be if there wasn't always someone watching her? Right now it all felt meaningless, and she grieved for all of the different paths she might have taken in her life. She was only in her early thirties, but it felt too late to start a new career. There had never been anything other than acting for her; she had no experience or training in anything else.

High school had been a very difficult time for her. Her family moved around a lot, and her shyness made it even harder to make friends. Acting became an unlikely lifeline. In high school, when she was staying in upstate New York with her grandfather, an English teacher named Mr. Kelly told her that her writing was good. He said that she was capable of doing well, if she would only apply herself. That teacher also ran the drama club, so she went along one day after school when he encouraged her toward it. Drama club sparked something in her, made her feel like a part of something special. The other kids there were all misfits too, and they were kind to her. There had always been an urge within her to reveal something of herself, even when she was feeling at her most guarded, and acting gave her the space to finally do that.

Despite her shyness, she had a stubbornness that paid off when she decided to act. Countless auditions and rejections couldn't discourage her, because she was used to feeling unwanted. There was nothing like the high she experienced when doors started to open for her.

But now that high was gone. She had made it, she was successful, and that success felt empty. She was a member of the in-crowd, yet she still felt like an outsider. There were times during her career when she had truly loved acting, but right now she couldn't remember the last time she felt that way. It was becoming difficult for her to find roles that she was passionate about. She was spending more and more of her time making movies like *Texas Twist*.

Though she had doubts about *Texas Twist*, she eventually managed to knuckle down and get to work. It wasn't in her nature to do a half-assed job whether she cared about the role or not. Studying the script became part of her morning routine, sandwiched between having her breakfast and taking Chester for a walk.

The day before rehearsals were due to start, there was a knock at the cottage door. Lauren jumped at the noise. Nobody had knocked on her door since she'd gotten there. She had become very used to her own company.

When she looked through the front window and saw Sal standing there, Lauren flung the door open.

"Sal, Sal, Sal. You never did learn how to use the phone did you?" she teased. She offered her cheek and Sal kissed her loudly, and then gave her a hug.

"Well, you didn't call me back last time I tried to call you, so I called Melinda to find out where you were. I hear you've become quite the hermit," he said. Sal pulled away and looked at her, inspecting her face for clues. "Everyone's worried about you. I've had your team on the phone to me more than once. You're okay, right?"

"Of course I'm okay. I've just been laying low for a while," Lauren said breezily. At some point during the last week she had become very relaxed, though she hadn't been conscious of the point where she clicked over into feeling so at ease. For the first time in a while, she felt happy and she was glad to see a familiar face to share it with.

"Well, it's time to stop that nonsense and strap in for the ride. I think this one's going to be my masterpiece," Sal announced, flopping down onto her sofa and stretching out his long legs.

Sal was a huge presence in more ways than one. He looked more like an aging rock star than a director. He had long hair that he tied into a ponytail, and he always wore black jeans and 70s punk band T-shirts. You would never know to look at him that he wrote fluffy, sentimental love stories. Lauren had known him for years, since back when they had traveled in the same independent movie circles. Sal had sold out even before she had.

Lauren laughed. "This film going to be the *Citizen Kane* of rom-coms."

Sal frowned. "That hurts me. Don't insult my art. I'm a sensitive man, and this shoot is already a disaster. Lori quit. It's a bad omen."

Lauren shook her head. "It's not a bad omen if it happens every five minutes and it's your fault. What did you do to her?"

Sal pulled a face that made it clear he was never going to tell her the answer to that question. Lauren had met Lori a couple of times, but she didn't know her well because Lori was the sixth or seventh assistant Sal had hired since Lauren had known him, mostly because he kept trying to sleep with them. Though Lauren disapproved of Sal's behavior at times, there was an authenticity and brutal honesty about him that she appreciated. He was very good at what he did.

"What do you think of this one-horse town? The tax breaks are amazing, the scenery is perfect for what I want to do, but there sure ain't much to do here," Sal said. "I got here yesterday, and I think I've already seen everything there is to see."

Lauren shrugged. "I don't mind it. I like the quiet. I'm glad you decided to write me a Southern belle part if it means I get out of the city for a while."

"Ha. I give you another week before you're dying to get back to the museums and restaurants. You can't live without that culture. You're a New York snob through and through."

Lauren frowned at him. "That's not true. I'm actually enjoying having a few home cooked meals. I like it here. The people are nice."

"Whatever. I'm worried that it's changed you. What the hell do you call those pants?" Sal pointed accusingly at her gray shorts. They were sweatpants that she'd cut the ends off because they would be far too warm otherwise. They were the most comfortable thing she had ever worn.

"Get used to them, I wear them nearly every day. I have two pairs."

"I'd better not see them on set. In fact, get them off right now and put on something presentable. I say we go down to this cute little place I found, have us a good, old-fashioned lunch date?" Sal suggested. "I found somewhere decent to eat here. It's a diner on the main strip. Good Southern cooking."

"You want to go to Joe's? I guess that would be okay," Lauren agreed, trying to sound neutral about the idea.

"How did you know where I was talking about? You mean you have actually left the house?"

"I've been outside once or twice you know." Lauren threw a cushion at him and moved to get ready.

They sat in the same booth where she had eaten during her last visit. A flash of red hair at the corner of her eye caught her attention, but Lauren tried to keep her eyes on Sal. He was talking about a certain executive that he hated, and how happy he was that they were shooting out here so that he could avoid him as much as possible. Sal loved the money he got to throw around on studio films but hated actually dealing with the studio.

Lauren had thought about Harper more than once since she had first seen her. Every now and then she would picture what it would be like to run into her on the street. She had also relived their last meeting several times in her mind, imagining it going very differently. In her revisions, Lauren hadn't been so socially awkward. Instead she had been effortlessly charming and cool in a way that she could never be in real life. Lauren thought that she had grown out of having crushes on straight women long ago, but she kept picturing those brown eyes and hearing the woman's beautiful lilting accent. It was embarrassing how happy she was that Harper was working today.

"You should see this cute piece that works here. Oh, there she is. I'm thinking about firing you and replacing you with big red over there." Sal pointed very indiscreetly toward Harper, and Lauren's face flushed. "Isn't she a knockout?"

Lauren glanced over at Harper and felt it again, that shock that came from seeing true beauty. Lauren quickly averted her eyes, intent on not making the same mistakes as she had last time.

"Jesus, Sal, do you ever think about anything else?"

"Never. Never ever," Sal affirmed, wiggling his thick eyebrows at her.

"Hi guys. Welcome. What can I get you folks?" Harper asked, smiling and looking back and forth between them.

Sal put his hand under his chin and grinned in a way that Lauren assumed was supposed to be cute. "*Folks.* I should get you to come down and coach some of my actors in how to do an authentic Southern accent. You really have a lovely way of speaking, has anyone ever told you that?"

"That's nice of you to say, but there's really nothing unique about the way I talk around here," Harper said, smiling and pausing expectantly with pen in hand. Something about the way she handled Sal made Lauren wonder if sleazy guys hit on her all the time.

"What do you think, Lauren? I bet your accent could do with a little work. Should we get Harper to come down to the set and show you a thing or two?"

Lauren shot him a look and shook her head slightly. She wasn't sure if the innuendo was deliberate or not, because you could never tell with him. The thought of Harper showing her things was tempting, but she could not let her mind go any further down that path. Lauren didn't want to think about what kind of impression she must be making on Harper. The first time they had met she could barely string a sentence together, and now she was here with a man who came across like a jerk. Lauren tried to force a smile, but she couldn't summon up much of one. She wished she hadn't come in here again, especially not with Sal.

"Could I have the salad please?" Lauren asked. The last thing she needed was anyone pestering her about her weight. Sal had never been shy about telling her if he thought she didn't look good.

Sal waved his hand toward Lauren. "Oh God, you actresses. Don't know how to eat properly. I'll have the cheeseburger and fries please, sweetheart." Sal ignored the glare Lauren shot across the table at him.

"No problem," Harper said, taking their menus. Lauren accidentally brushed her fingers against Harper's. Harper pulled her hand away quickly, but not before Lauren had noticed the long and finely shaped fingers and felt the jolt as their skin connected.

The smile fell from Harper's face before she turned to leave. Lauren watched until Harper was safely out of earshot. "Sal, could you please try to be less of a dick?"

"Oh don't be that way. She didn't mind. You never answered me. Do you think she's hot?"

"Just stop it," Lauren said.

Although Sal was aware of her sexuality, there was no way she could feel comfortable talking about Harper like that. It was an open secret within a very small circle that she dated women, but she kept the details mainly to herself. Celia and Franklin, two of the people who had helped shepherd her career from the start, were always warning her about how coming out could damage her career. Lauren usually confined her interest to women who were in the industry. It meant that they had as much to lose from any publicity as she did. It wasn't the ideal way to conduct a relationship, though, and most of them only lasted for a month or two.

Sighing, Harper approached the kitchen. Sue was looking at her with narrowed eyes.

"It's not fair, why are they always sitting in your section?" Sue asked. "That guy was at the same table yesterday."

"Sorry Sue, it's just luck. It'll go your way tomorrow, maybe," Harper said.

Despite the extra money the diner was making and the tips she was earning, Harper would be happier when all these people left. Lauren made her uneasy. There was a dismissive manner that made her feel small, like Lauren didn't think she was worth even talking to or looking at. Harper wasn't sure why the way Lauren treated her mattered so much. In a sense, Lauren's attitude had nothing to do with her, because it wasn't like they knew one another at all. Harper liked to think she didn't care about the movie stuff that Sue thought was so important, but maybe she did.

The next morning, Sal came in early to buy coffee. She knew he was the director of the movie because he had bragged about it the first day he came in. Sal appeared to be the type of man who was used to charming people and always got what he wanted. The less attention Harper gave him, the more he chased after her. She had met men like him before. It was of no use telling them that she preferred women, because it only made them chase after her even more. Harper knew she had to treat Sal with a cool attitude rather than give him any ammunition at all.

When Harper handed him his change, he touched her hand for a second in a familiar way, and she pulled it away. The hand was placed firmly out of reach in the pocket of her uniform.

"No getting fresh, sir, or I'll get you thrown out of here," she said, half joking but seriously enough that he would know not to try it again.

"Sorry. Listen, I was thinking. Do you think you can get time off from here? I happen to be hiring right now," he said, holding the hot cardboard cup in both hands.

Harper raised her eyebrows. Men like him really would try anything if the challenge seemed great enough. "What are you talking about? I don't know anything at all about the movie business. Do you need someone to serve food or something?"

"Nope, I don't want you to do craft service. You would be working for me. You seem smart, quick on your feet," Sal said.

"You've learned all that from me bringing you coffee a couple of times?" she asked.

Sal held his arms out. "I'm a very good judge of character. My personal assistant quit and I really want to get another one before we start shooting. I could do with someone temporary until I get back home and can hire someone else. I'd pay you well. You don't need any training, it's just managing things for me here and there. I'm sure you can learn it on the job."

"I'd need to think about it," Harper said. It was a strange

offer and she would be stupid if she didn't see why he was making it. Who would just offer a job without an interview or any idea of what she could actually do?

"Here, take my card." As Sal handed over the small piece of cardboard, he held onto the edge of it for a second. "I don't just give this out to anyone."

Harper put the card in the pocket of her dress without looking at it. Sal nodded at her once more and walked out.

Sue, who had been lingering behind them, came running over to her. "Did I just hear what I think I heard? Did he offer you a job?"

"Yep. It's crazy right? He must think I was born yesterday," Harper said.

"You're not going to do it? Why the hell not?"

"Because he's a sleazy scumbag?"

"You are so boring. Why don't you just give it a try? The rest of us would kill for an opportunity like that." Sue walked away muttering to herself. Harper looked guiltily at her back.

Harper stewed about Sal's proposal and Sue's reaction to it all night. Maybe she had never pictured herself doing a job like the one Sal was asking her to do, but then she hadn't pictured herself working at the diner forever either. The extra money he mentioned was difficult to refuse. Harper had been trying so hard to keep them all afloat, but by the time they paid the bills and her dad bought his whiskey and cigarettes, there wasn't a whole lot left over. If she ever wanted to start her life again, it would help to have some cash saved up.

Maybe it wouldn't hurt just to try it. She called Sal the next day. When he came on the line, she abruptly told him her terms. "I'm not going to sleep with you. If you make rude comments to me or if I get the slightest hint that you're only hiring me for a bit of fun, I'll walk out immediately and sue for sexual harassment. I know the law, and I know a lot of lawyers too."

There was a stunned silence, and then he laughed. "We're going to get along just fine. I like you. When can you start?"

CHAPTER FOUR

When Harper arrived for the first day of her new job, her heart was thudding. The address Sal gave her was for an old warehouse on the outskirts of town. It had once been the home of Hanson's Cannery, a business that went under before she was even born. There was paint flaking from the walls. The vacant lot next to it had been turned into a car park for expensive vehicles that looked very out of place next to the crab grasses and abandoned car parts that littered the ground.

Harper was nowhere near sure that she had made the right decision about this. She had to keep telling herself that she had done nothing irreversible, and that she could quit if this turned out to be as crazy as it seemed. It was an overnight career change. Though it went against her sense of herself as a responsible person, she hadn't even given two weeks' notice. Her boss Ben told her that his niece was on a break from school, so he could just get her in for a couple of months to cover.

Harper's father had been quietly shocked when she'd told him about her plans. Like her, he had ignored the stories about the movie shooting in town, so he had to ask her a number of questions before he understood what she was talking about. It had been a long time since he was in a position to offer her fatherly guidance, so he didn't have much else to say about it. He congratulated her on the new job and went back to his TV show, though she saw the slight quizzical frown on his face when he did it.

Harper wandered around, searching for Sal's office. The partitioning of rooms with cheap wood had created thin hallways, making the whole place into a rabbit warren. A couple of people passed her in the hall, but nobody stopped her to ask who she was or what she was doing there.

Sal's door was marked with a big sheet of paper with his name on it. It swung open when she knocked.

"Oh, thank God you're here, I need coffee. Would you get something for me to eat with it too?" Sal said in a rush. Harper was relieved at being asked to do something she actually knew how to do. Until he spoke to her, she had been half expecting to be told that this was all a big practical joke.

It made her feel a little sheepish to go back into the diner. She resisted the urge to clean up a table covered in dirty napkins set on top of a lonely plate. When Sue teased her about not being able to stay away from the diner, Harper told her that it was just as well seeing as the place was a mess. It felt good to walk in there, but it felt just as good to walk out, and to know that she wasn't going to be stuck inside there all day.

When she got back to the warehouse she found Sal sitting in the middle of the room, leading a meeting.

"Is she going to take all the best lines again? Are you going to let her suck up all my screen time?" Josh was asking.

Harper recognized the movie's leading man thanks to Sue and her crush. Sue had been shoving pictures from magazines in Harper's face for weeks now, trying to educate her about the film. Josh was very conventionally handsome, with chiseled cheekbones and a prominent jawline. Josh, Sal, Lauren and a woman that Harper didn't recognize all had scripts in their laps.

"You are so full of it. You know that's not what happened," Lauren said. She reached down for a second toward the small, fluffy black dog that was curled around her ankles, and scratched its head absently. Like everyone else in the room, the dog did not notice that Harper was there.

"Are you two going to be teasing one other like this the whole shoot? I'm not sure I have the energy," Sal said.

"I need to keep him in line, he's the one already acting like a world-class diva."

Because nobody was looking at her, Harper took a moment to study Lauren. It wasn't difficult to believe that she was a movie star. She somehow shone brighter than other people and projected a strong presence even when she wasn't speaking.

"You're the only diva around here, I think you'll find."

Lauren rolled her eyes and then, apparently feeling eyes on her, she looked up at Harper. She stared at Harper's face impassively.

"See, look at this. My notes say I could drop this line here about my mom. I don't think we need it. Does that sound like I'm trying to beef up my role?" Lauren said, her eyes moving down Harper's body before returning to the script.

Harper looked down at her own outfit, sure that Lauren had just been judging the way she was dressed. It had not been easy to decide what to wear this morning. Harper was accustomed to her waitress's uniform. She hadn't needed to think about what to wear to work for a long time. Eventually, she had chosen a skirt and blouse that she'd found in the back of her closet from back when she'd worked in the city. When she tried the clothes on, she had thought she looked professional but not too dressed up. Now that she was here, she could see there was no real dress code. Nobody would think twice if she wore jeans. Harper looked straight ahead of her, making sure she didn't look at Lauren again.

Finally, Sal beckoned her to come closer. She handed him his coffee and sandwich.

"Thanks, sweetheart," Sal said. Harper gave him a warning look but decided to let it go for now, knowing it would be a bad move to say anything when there were so many people around. But he needed to know that they weren't at the diner anymore. Lauren's eyes were on her again; she could feel it.

"What would you like me to do now?" Harper asked.

Sal waved his hand at her. "Take it easy on your first day, I don't need much. Go around and introduce yourself, take a look at how things run. To begin with, this is Loretta, the script supervisor. You've met Lauren, and this is Josh, my leading man."

Harper shook hands with Loretta and then with Josh.

"I'll come and find you when we're done, and I'll take you through some stuff," Sal said.

Harper nodded and closed the door behind her, standing with her hand pressed to it for a moment. Sal seemed like a very relaxed boss, which didn't actually sit that well with her. She didn't like the idea of just floating around without any direction. Harper stopped short of pulling the door all the way shut. It was still open half an inch or so. She could hear someone laughing and guessed that it must be Lauren. There was a sarcastic edge to it, and she knew with a sinking feeling that they were all talking about her. Harper quickly looked around to make sure there was nobody else out in the hallway, and then stood close to the door so she could hear properly.

"What are you doing, Sal?"

"What? I needed an assistant."

"So you recruited from the local diner?"

"She's clearly smart and competent. I think she'll be great."

"That may be the case, but it's obviously not why you hired her."

Harper resented the statement, not to mention the way the other people in the room laughed as though they agreed with it.

"I used the resources available to me. What was I supposed to do? Halt production and fly back to LA to hire someone? I don't have time to worry about things like that." Sal sounded bored, like he couldn't be bothered arguing.

"You know you could have arranged someone to do that *for* you, and had a real assistant out on the next plane. You're such a pig."

"Why do you care who my assistant is?" Sal replied.

"I don't care. But there was no need to go out and buy yourself a toy to play with while we're supposed to be working," Lauren snapped. "You just use them up and throw them away, it's not nice."

Harper stepped away from the door. She didn't need to hear any more, given how uncomfortable she was around Lauren already. It was a mystery why Lauren was so hostile toward her when they had barely interacted. Harper usually had a pretty thick skin, but Lauren's comments were upsetting. She wanted to believe that Sal really had only hired her for the reasons he had just mentioned, and not because he wanted to get into her pants. It was so humiliating to hear her fears being articulated by someone else like they were a fact.

Harper turned and walked away down the hall. Nobody else might know it, but she was ridiculously overqualified for this role. She could run errands for Sal standing on her head. She was determined to act professionally, and to show Lauren and everyone else that she was more than worthy of being here.

Over the next few days, Harper threw herself into her work, and was surprised at how much she enjoyed it. It was low in responsibility, but fun for her to have such a varied role. She was given a small office with a desk and computer so she had a base from which to answer Sal's emails and take phone calls. She spent a lot of time running around doing whatever Sal asked her to do, but at least it was never boring.

Harper had never given a lot of thought to how movies were made, or to how many people were involved. There were whole professions that she'd never imagined existing. They were preparing a bunch of locations around town, in houses and ranches and old empty buildings. Someone explained to her that Sal had wanted everything to be as natural as possible, and that was why it was all happening right here in town rather than on a soundstage. There were days when she would ride along in vans and watch as it all came together. It was fascinating.

The only downside of her new job was there were long periods during which there wasn't a lot for her to do. She had quickly learned that making movies meant a lot of waiting around. Sal didn't seem to care how she spent her time as long as she was around when he needed something. She made the best of the situation, downloading law journals and reading articles so that she could keep up with changes. It had been a long time since she had done much reading. It was good to feel stimulated in the way the law made her feel. When she tired of that and needed a break, she would read books or the gossip magazines Sue had always foisted off on her and that she had never cracked open before.

During one of her quiet times, she was flipping through one of the magazines. She had glanced at the front page and somehow managed to miss the picture of Lauren in the corner. When she turned to the article she saw a big pink headline that said, "Lauren's Ultimatum: Marry Me or It's Splits Ville." There was a picture of Lauren and Josh walking through an airport with blank expressions on their faces beneath their sunglasses.

Harper's eyebrows went up but only slightly. She had not had any idea that Josh and Lauren were a couple, but then why would she? There was nothing that surprising about it anyway. The most shocking thing about it was that Sue hadn't mentioned it to her in all that time she was mooning over Josh.

Now that she was thinking about Lauren, she looked up the app she'd downloaded in an attempt to learn a bit more about movies. She had looked up Sal's entry so far, but nothing else. She wanted to jog her memory about that movie she had seen so long ago, the one she thought about when she found out who Lauren was. Harper typed in Lauren's name to bring up her filmography. The movie was *Edge of the Sea*. She recognized the name now that she saw it, and more details came flooding back.

When she looked up the blurb, Harper noticed that Lauren had her only co-writing credit on the film. When Harper looked through the list of movies she had done, it looked as though Lauren's career had changed course not long after that movie came out. There was a string of fluffy-looking titles right after it, names that she vaguely recognized. She wondered why Lauren had never written anything else.

Harper was still browsing the list of credits when Sal called her to his office. Distractedly, he handed her a page of notes to deliver to the wardrobe designer, Sherri. Sal had assistant directors who were often out at various locations, so running around to deliver instructions sometimes fell to her. By now Harper had learned her way around, so she easily located the wardrobe department. When she stepped inside, she looked around at racks and racks of clothing and mannequins, taking a moment to find the main floor where Sherri was working.

"Hey guys," Harper said, feeling a twinge of guilt when she realized the person she had just been stalking via her filmography was in the room with Sherri. Lauren was standing on a raised block while Sherri kneeled at her feet.

"Hey Harper," Sherri said warmly, taking pins out of her mouth to speak. They had met a couple of times, and Harper really liked Sherri. She was a warm older woman, who always looked stylish in an eccentric way.

Harper started to smile back at her but stopped when she glanced behind Sherri and met Lauren's eyes. Lauren was standing with her arms crossed over her chest. Harper just now realized that she was clad only in a skirt and black bra. Harper also noticed, with a flush of embarrassment, just how perfect Lauren's body was.

When she glanced back up at Lauren's face, she saw that it was red, and Harper wasn't sure whether it was due to anger or embarrassment.

"I'm sorry," Harper said.

"It would be great if you could knock before you come in," Lauren said, more gently than Harper expected.

"Of course, I'll do that in future," Harper said, trying to sound diligent and eager to please, like this was just another direction that someone had given her.

What was she supposed to do now? Lauren's green eyes never left hers. She realized they'd never made eye contact for such a long time, though they had come close that first day in the diner. She was used to Lauren's gaze slipping away, like her eyes didn't know what to catch on.

This was different. It felt like it was only the two of them in the room. There was something in the way that Lauren stared at her that made her feel like she was exposed too.

"Um, can I..." she said, flailing and shifting her focus to Sherri. It seemed wise to put her energy into not looking at Lauren at all.

"Oh sure, hon, just put them on the floor over here," Sherri said. Harper nodded and set the papers down, aware of Lauren's gaze following her the whole time.

"Thanks, sweetie," Sherri said, oblivious to the undercurrent in the room.

Harper walked out knowing that she was only going to be more uneasy around Lauren from now on. It made her feel strange, that she had felt that powerful of an attraction toward someone she neither liked nor respected. It was as though something were happening between them, like Lauren had known what she was thinking. She had noticed the curve of Lauren's breasts, and the way her body tapered in at the waist.

Harper tried to put the thoughts out of her head. Lauren wasn't a mind reader, and in fact probably was too self-absorbed to give much thought to her at all.

CHAPTER FIVE

It unsettled Lauren that Sal had brought Harper into her workplace. She always became anxious at the start of a shoot, when she was still getting to know everyone and figuring out who was who. This time it helped that she had already worked with Sal and Josh, but she hadn't expected to have Harper walking past her in the halls and into meetings. Avoiding Harper by staying away from the diner had been relatively easy. This was not.

It threw her just a little bit off balance every time Harper walked into a room. She strode around with her shoulders back and her hips swaying, ready to take on whatever might be thrown at her. When Lauren examined the sense of intimidation she felt, she knew that it wasn't just about the pull of desire toward Harper. It was the way Harper carried herself, the way she was so sure of who she was. Being around her made Lauren feel weak and even more shy than usual. All the relaxation she had done in the lead up to the shoot had gone to waste. She was back to being tightly wound again. She found herself doling out tight smiles and stiff greetings if she had to speak to Harper at all.

The truth was that Lauren really wanted to get to know Harper better and just couldn't bring herself to do it. Her curiosity increased each time Sal talked about how whip-smart she was, how interesting and easy to get along with she was. Sometimes it felt like all Lauren wanted was for Harper to like her and to be seen by her, but it would be dangerous to open herself up like that and risk rejection. She was fearful that if she got to know Harper any more, she would only want her more.

The sense of holding herself back was nothing new for her. Early in her career, Lauren had made the decision that she would never come out. Cultivating an image was a game that everybody played. It had never occurred to her that she could play it differently. Very few of her colleagues were openly gay. Those who were out stuck to the indies and the occasional guest role on a television show. At first, she had dodged the subject of her private life. It had been easy when there were few people asking her questions. As she became more successful, her manager Celia and publicist Franklin prepared answers that she recited. She would say that she had no interest in talking about her life because she wanted to completely disappear into her roles. That approach only worked for a short time. The higher her profile rose, the more the media wanted to peek into every corner of her life.

Finally, and only after quite a lot of pressure, Lauren allowed Franklin to circulate stories about her dating men. He explained to her from the start that it was no big deal, that they did it about everyone regardless of sexuality. In interviews she covered her fear by trying to project an air of mystery, answering questions vaguely so that people could think whatever they wanted. When she read anything about herself, it was laughable how much of it was made up. Every article noted how intriguing and aloof and guarded she was.

When she met a woman she found attractive, the first question that always came to mind was: who would the woman tell? Lauren always worried about rumors getting out. The one time Lauren had been less than discreet, she had suffered for it. The relationship with Angela—and its horrific, embarrassing aftermath—was not an experience she ever wanted to repeat. She'd trusted Angela. She was unlikely to ever trust anyone like that again. Lauren never really felt that strongly for the woman who betrayed her, but that didn't make it any better. She now knew what it felt like to have her privacy breached but she had never experienced a violation like that. The worst aspect of it was that she only had herself to blame.

So now, Chester was all that she was willing to have for company, and that was fine by her. She spent every night lying on the couch with him watching movies. Since she'd arrived in Texas, she had socialized only as much as she'd wanted to. There had been a drink with Sal, and she had gone for a drive with Sherri and couple of women from the wardrobe department. It wasn't anything like living in New York or working in Los Angeles. There were no industry events to go to on Saturday nights and no pretentious nightclubs to be seen in. She had always found that aspect of her job tiring. It was a relief to be away from it all.

It had been a long time since she'd immersed herself in cinema. When she was growing up, movies were so important to her. They were an escape, a way to feel less alone. As a kid, she'd practically lived at the video store. It was a part of herself that she'd lost touch with, despite her career. Now she had a chance to get back into it, to watch all those old classics she loved so much. She wished she could have been a part of it all back then, when things were so glamorous. So safe.

Lauren had developed a Sunday routine that she was completely in love with. She would throw open the curtains so she could look out at the leafy trees outside of her bedroom window, then get up to make a pot of coffee. After that, she would go back to bed and curl up with a book with Chester snuggled against her legs. When she got so hungry she had no choice but to get up, she would hit the kitchen and make a big breakfast. She would eat it on the back porch and enjoy the sunshine and quiet, the only noise coming from the birds. Then it would be time to take Chester out for a walk.

She had been slowly exploring the surrounding areas near her cottage, and finding out just how many lovely parks you could cram into one town. Chester would bound ahead of her, smelling the ground or running up to people, then return to her. Over time, Lauren had gotten used to strangers saying their friendly hellos to her, and occasionally she'd stop for a quick chat. Most people made it very easy for her—they loved hearing about how much she was enjoying being in town. So many people had offered to show her around that she had lost count, but nobody seemed offended when she declined.

That day, she was walking through a tree-lined park she had found close to home. She picked up a stick and threw it for Chester. He eagerly chased it down on his short little legs and brought it back to her.

"You are such a good little dog Chester. You know I'm wild about you, don't you? You know I love you the best right?" she said, ruffling his curly hair. He panted up at her. "And you're smart too. You understand human English, don't you?"

Lauren stood up and looked ahead of her, taking in the clean, fresh air. Days like this made her so happy. They filled her with the conviction that her life was getting better. Her anxiety and her fears were miles away, tucked safely back in the city where they belonged. She stood for a moment, feeling content to not have to be anywhere in particular. Chester ran away from her, sniffing the earth. There was a woman in his path, lying motionless on the grass, with her elbow thrown across her eyes. Her pose suggested that she was gloriously comfortable. Some people had a gift for looking at home in whichever environment they were in. Lauren wished she had that quality herself.

With a spark of excitement, Lauren thought she might see red hair. Later, she was unsure why she had walked toward someone that she had been so carefully avoiding. Maybe it had something to do with how at ease she felt in that moment. The woman had looked like she was sleeping, so it hadn't felt like it mattered that much.

Lauren intended to keep a wide berth, but Chester had other ideas. She hadn't kept him on a leash today and he ran directly toward the person she was now absolutely sure was Harper.

"Chester!" she called as quietly as she could, but it was too late. He was sniffing around Harper, who abruptly came to life and sat up. Lauren watched, hanging back, while Harper looked at Chester for a moment and then started patting him. He walked around in a circle and then settled down onto Harper's lap.

Harper looked toward Lauren and smiled as though a strange dog jumping all over her was the most natural thing in the world. There was a fluttering in Lauren's stomach as she hesitantly walked forward.

"Hey. He's cute. How old is he?" Harper asked her.

"Five, even though he acts like a puppy," Lauren said, having to search for the words.

Harper scratched under Chester's jaw. She looked up for a second at Lauren, who was standing uncertainly trying to decide whether to try to cajole Chester away or not. "You can sit if you want to."

Although she doubted that it was a genuine invitation, Lauren moved closer and knelt down, resting on her knees. She noticed now that Harper was wearing running shorts and a tank top, and that there was sweat across her collarbone. "I'm sorry that he disturbed you."

"It's not a problem."

"Were you sleeping?" Lauren said, knowing that it was a stupid thing to ask as soon as it came out of her mouth.

Harper looked at her kindly, which somehow made her feel even more exposed. "It's really okay. I was just resting."

Neither of them said anything for a while, and Lauren was thankful that Chester was there to act as a buffer. He had rolled onto his back and Harper scratched his stomach while his little paws flailed in the air.

Lauren finally thought of a question she could ask. "How are you finding it? Working for Sal I mean?"

"Fine, why?" Harper asked.

Lauren detected an undercurrent in Harper's answer, a tone she didn't understand. She got the feeling that maybe Harper didn't like her asking that question. It had only been a week since Harper had started working for him. She hoped Sal hadn't already done anything to cause issues.

"No reason," said Lauren. "I just know that he can be a bit... Sal's a good friend of mine, but he can be inappropriate sometimes."

"Yeah, he can be kind of interesting," Harper replied cautiously.

"He can be a jerk. Let's just say that he's a little like Chester. Without careful training he'll try to jump all over your lap," Lauren blurted out. She faltered on the last word but it didn't matter, because Harper's laugh was genuine. The way she laughed, so openly and infectiously, made Lauren's heart beat faster. She hadn't been sure whether she should even make the joke, but it had paid off.

"I was hoping people didn't think there was something going on between us, with the way he acts," Harper said with relief.

"I didn't think that. I just know Sal sometimes get a bit confused about what's okay and what's plain old sexual harassment. I hope I'm not being presumptuous if I tell you it's okay to just tell him straight. He'll get it eventually."

"Oh he knows how I feel already, but thanks. Really," Harper said. She looked up and smiled at Lauren, and then went back to rubbing Chester's stomach. Lauren tried to think of something else to say, but was at a loss.

"Hey, I've been meaning to tell you," said Harper. "I saw you in *Edge of the Sea* when it came out. It was really good."

Lauren flushed in surprise. That movie was her favorite thing that she had ever done. It would always be special to her because she had co-written the script with her friend Christine. It had a cult following, though it had not been successful by any other measure. It never led to serious roles like she'd hoped, but it had made the industry take note of her and she got a lot of meetings after it came out. When people approached her it was usually about one of her more popular movies, but she always appreciated the ones who commented on *Edge of the Sea* the most.

"Thank you. That's so nice of you to say." Another awkward silence followed, although Harper didn't seem to mind it. Her attention was on Chester, who'd started licking her hand.

"I should get home. I've been here way longer than I should have. I didn't mean to doze off like that," Harper said.

"I can understand why you did. This place is so relaxing, and it's such a beautiful day."

"It really is." Harper patted Chester affectionately.

"C'mon Chester, let's let Harper get home. I'll see you soon."

"See you at work."

As Harper walked away, she smiled and waved good-bye again over her shoulder. Lauren stood watching her for longer than she should have, her heart skipping like a stone.

CHAPTER SIX

Harper had never considered it a failing on her part that she sometimes missed things about others. She was the sort of person who wore her heart on her sleeve; she'd even been told that she could be honest to a fault. It seemed that her own forthrightness made her assume she could take everyone else at face value. It was times like these that she wished she were more adept at reading people.

It had never occurred to her that Lauren might be acting aloof because she was just shy. When Lauren approached her in the park and it was just the two of them, Harper easily picked up on the way Lauren fidgeted uncomfortably. Now and then Lauren's voice would trail off like she wasn't sure of what she was saying, and her gaze would slide away self-consciously.

Harper now realized that Lauren had said those things about her to Sal because she disapproved of his behavior. The criticism had been aimed squarely at him. Lauren had been acting protectively toward her, which struck her as incredibly sweet.

It all made Harper see Lauren in a different light. Lauren was nothing like Harper had assumed. There was a kindness in her that Harper had missed. Now that she knew better, any hostility toward Lauren completely dropped away. It was a relief, because she had been dreading her interactions with Lauren. For a few days, that feeling had been the only thing she hadn't liked about her job. When she went to work the next day she felt lighter, like things were going to be better from now on.

Just as Harper was getting to her office door, she heard Lauren's voice greeting her from a few feet away.

"Good morning," Lauren said. "Did you enjoy the rest of your day yesterday?"

Harper paused with her hand on the doorknob. When she looked over her shoulder, she saw Lauren standing there, a sweet half smile on her face. The question sounded formal, like Lauren had rehearsed what she was going to say.

"I did, thanks. It was very relaxing. What about you?"

Lauren took a while to answer. "I had a good day, thanks."

"Did you want to come in and hang out for a while?" Harper asked, trying to put Lauren at ease.

Lauren's smile turned up to its full potential and she shook her head. "I'm on my way to another wardrobe fitting. Thank you, though."

As she walked away, Harper watched her for a moment. There it was again, that shyness and the sense that it was hard for Lauren to talk to her. It was as though Lauren was really putting herself out there just to say hello to someone that she didn't know very well. Harper reflected that it must be a difficult way to go through life. It was strange that someone so painfully shy had chosen an acting career, of all things. If it was difficult for Lauren to talk to *her*, a complete nobody, then what must it be like going on TV and doing interviews and all that stuff?

That night when she went home, she was determined to get her hands on Lauren's old movie. The urge to watch *Edge of the Sea* had been nagging at Harper ever since she had looked it up, and it only got stronger since she and Lauren spoke the day before. Harper tried to download it but wasn't able to find it.

There was a store in the next town over that she thought might have the DVD, so she called them to see if they stocked it. The bored-sounding teenager who answered the phone said flatly that he'd never heard of it, but eventually he came back to the phone and said they had it.

She drove over and picked it up. Initially she was planning to watch only the first half hour, but got so absorbed in it that she finished it. The film was as good as she had remembered. It was funny and poignant, and she found herself moved by it once again.

For moments she would get lost in the story and then with a jolt she would remember that it was Lauren she was seeing. Harper didn't know much about acting, but it seemed like Lauren completely disappeared into the character. The woman on the screen had a different voice that was clearer and stronger. When she walked, she moved with a straight spine and her chin thrust forward. Harper shifted awkwardly on the sofa when Lauren disrobed for a love scene with her male co-star. There wasn't much skin on display, save for Lauren's toned back and shoulders, but she looked at the actor with a desire real enough to make Harper feel like a voyeur. Harper remembered that after they had seen it, she and her friend had exclaimed over how attractive Lauren was. It made her uncomfortable to think about that now.

When she went to work the next day, she was bleary-eyed from staying up late to finish the movie. She was hoping to have one of those quiet days where Sal would leave her to her own devices, but instead he called her in early. Harper was aware that Sal, Lauren, Josh, and various other players were having meetings to work out last-minute problems with the script. Although she had never been present for the entirety of one of their meetings, she often heard fragments of conversations as she came and went. The discussions usually sounded heated, with Sal's and Josh's voices rising passionately while Lauren's quiet voice came out from underneath them.

"I just don't understand what the issue is here," Sal was saying when she entered.

Harper skirted around the edge of the room in an effort to be unobtrusive. She handed a mug of coffee to each of them. Lauren was the only one who smiled at her in acknowledgment. In the seconds after Lauren turned her attention back to Sal and Josh, Harper felt something she hadn't anticipated. She wanted Lauren to keep looking at her.

"Because I think you're going to turn off half the audience with this, Sal. More than half, if you consider that this movie is supposed to be aimed mainly at women," Lauren said.

"I'm not sure," Josh said, frowning. "I don't know what I think about this."

"I've written a lot of these things, Lauren, very successfully I might add. I know what my audience wants. The studio loved the script, so stop trying to rewrite *my* movie," Sal said.

"I'm not trying to do that," Lauren countered.

"We all know you can write, but this one is not yours."

Lauren shook her head. "You know I know better than that, Sal. I never try to rewrite anything. You said you wanted to workshop this scene. I'm just giving you the opinion you asked for."

Harper stood to the side and waited patiently for further instructions. She had come to understand that when she was in a room with Sal and other people, she was a low priority for a while. Eventually, when he'd put out whatever fires he was dealing with at the time, Sal would tell her what he needed.

Sal threw up an arm. "Then explain it to me. What's the problem?"

"It's the whole premise of the scene," said Lauren calmly. "It makes my character out to be dopey and Josh's to be controlling."

"Hey, some women like that," Josh said. Sal didn't catch the sarcasm and nodded enthusiastically.

Lauren rolled her eyes at the two of them. "As the only woman taking part in this conversation, I'm telling you there are many women who would not enjoy getting treated this way. It's not romantic. I'm sorry to tell you this, Sal, but it's almost a bit offensive."

Sal clicked his fingers at Harper, who jumped slightly. "Second opinion? Harper, you're a woman. Let's put this to a vote."

"Oh I don't really..." Harper hesitated. The last thing she wanted was to get involved in a dispute over something she knew nothing about. What did she know about scripts or movies?

Sal ignored her objection. "Let me lay it out for you. So, you know that Josh's character is this big Texan oil magnate and Lauren's character is this good-hearted poor girl. In this scene, they're out on a date and Lauren is dressed up. She looks fantastic but she can't afford much. He offers to buy her a new wardrobe, but the way he offers is not insulting. It's like, what's the line Josh?"

"I want to buy you something that you're worthy of. Something as beautiful as you are. You deserve for the whole world to see you like I do," Josh read mechanically, then looked up at Harper. "If a guy said that to you, would you know how he meant it? It's not supposed to be an insult. When we do the scene I won't play it like that at all."

Harper squirmed as three sets of eyes looked at her expectantly. She didn't know anything about movies but it certainly sounded like something that would make her cringe if she saw it played out onscreen.

"Well...I'm not the person to answer that question," she deflected.

"Why not? Just imagine yourself in that position, like if a dude said that to you," Josh persisted. "It's chivalrous or whatever."

"I wouldn't be in that position," Harper replied. "So I don't know."

"Don't be obtuse. It's a movie. Maybe you wouldn't be exactly in that position but you can understand what we're saying. It's a fantasy. Imagine if Josh here offered to sweep you off your feet," Sal said. Josh helpfully put his hand under his chin and smoldered at her.

Harper looked around the room. Growing up in a small town, the assumption that she must like men always had more of an influence over her life than she wanted. In some ways, it was understandable, and she could never forget that she was a member of a minority. But it exasperated her all the same. Oftentimes she didn't bother to correct people when they treated her like she was heterosexual, but with all of them pressing her like this it felt like her only way out.

"No, I'm saying, I don't even date guys," Harper clarified. "So I really can't help you on this one. I'm not really an expert on the boy-girl thing. I'm not exactly your target demographic for this, I don't think."

"Oh," Sal said, nodding.

Harper glanced over at Lauren, who appeared to have just stopped short of doing a spit-take into her coffee. Did Lauren think she was sharing too much personal information? Harper didn't think of it that way anymore, not after spending time in New York where nobody cared. She had long since come out to her friends and family. The notion that sexuality had to be a private affair had always bothered her, especially when the idea never seemed to apply to people who were heterosexual. Where possible, she treated it like just another fact about herself.

"So you see, I can't help you out," Harper elaborated when nobody said anything.

"Oh that's nonsense, you're still a woman aren't you?" Sal said, unfazed. "Actually you're the perfect person to ask because you probably know women better than I do. Forget about Josh, let's say that it was Lauren who offered you all that stuff. Lauren's practically down on bended knee telling you that you're beautiful, that she wants to give you everything."

Harper deliberately didn't look in Lauren's direction. An image flashed through her mind of Lauren doing just that. Lauren's upturned face, the gaze toward Harper open and unafraid. Harper pushed it away.

Harper could see that despite her best efforts she wasn't going to be able to wriggle out of the situation. She took a moment to choose her words carefully. "With all due respect to you, Sal, I have to agree with Lauren. It doesn't send a great message. I'd be crushed if I got all ready for a date and that was the reaction to what I was wearing. I would want someone who liked me for who I already am and not what they could change me into. I think deep down that's what everyone wants."

Harper looked at the three of them, each sitting there with their faces turned toward her. Her eyes caught on Lauren's.

"That's exactly what I was trying to say," Lauren chimed in gratefully. Lauren smiled, and Harper returned it.

"Okay," Sal said reluctantly. "You do put it persuasively. Maybe you're right. We could find another way to get my point across. Okay, thanks Harper. I'll call you back in here later when we're done," he said, rubbing his hands together as though he was excited to get to work.

Before Harper walked out, she took one more glance at Lauren. Lauren was still smiling at her, but her eyes quickly dropped. Harper was used to that by now, but she had noticed that there was an appraising quality to her stare this time. Maybe she was trying to fit the new information about Harper into her concept of who Harper was. She was used to people being surprised and looking at her differently when they found out she was gay, so it was nothing new. At least now the information was out there and there could be no misunderstandings.

Harper's job became busier when they started filming. Sal's demeanor changed as his stress levels went up, and she had to get used to him barking orders at her. Her job was mainly comprised of replying to messages from the people at the studio, who Sal seemed very much invested in avoiding. She also spent her days going to get him things that seemed unimportant to her but that he claimed he needed. Half the time when she brought whatever it was, he had already lost interest by the time she got there. Once he sent her on an hour-long drive to find him a brand of soda that he was feeling nostalgic for, but she saw the unopened can sitting on his desk a day later.

Harper often ran around delivering recent changes to scenes because Sal was constantly tinkering with the script. Harper had found out that Sal was neurotic about locking in lines and always wanted to change them at the last minute right before filming a scene. People often groaned when she passed them yet another new set of pages.

They were shooting out on location at a local farmhouse, and Sal asked her to go and see Lauren in the hair and makeup trailer with some new pages. When she walked in, they didn't notice her at first. Lauren and the woman bent down toward her were laughing over something.

"Seriously, where are you flying with all that baggage under your eyes? You look like crap," the makeup woman said, dipping her finger into lotion and applying it to Lauren's skin. Ordinarily Harper would have assumed she was being rude, but it was obvious from Lauren's laughter that it was all in good fun.

"Just cover it up. Isn't that what they're paying you for?" Lauren said. She jumped at Harper's movement, which must have caught her eye in the mirror.

"Oh hey, Harper," Lauren said, slightly breathless.

Harper's eyes met Lauren's reflection, and Lauren smiled warmly at her. Harper didn't know what the makeup lady was talking about. She wouldn't have covered up a thing.

"Hey, I'm sorry to interrupt. Sal asked me to give you these."

"Don't tell me," Lauren said, taking the paper-clipped pages from Harper. "It's a rewrite of today's scene. And to think I had those lines down cold. I really don't know why I bother."

"Sorry to be the bearer of bad news," Harper replied.

Harper could barely keep the smile off her face when she spoke to Lauren lately. Perhaps it was because Lauren had come across as withholding for so long. If Lauren could converse with her in the easy way she was right now, it meant that they had gotten somewhere.

"Who are you?" the makeup person interrupted them, looking back and forth between Harper and Lauren.

"Oh, I'm sorry Martha. You haven't met yet? This is Sal's new assistant, Harper," Lauren introduced them. "And Harper, this is Martha, who, as you can see, is doing my makeup. We've worked together before. She's a wizard."

Martha looked Harper up and down. "You're a striking one. I thought you were in the movie for a second. You sure you're not?"

Harper flushed. Martha seemed like one of those outgoing people who never had a self-conscious moment, but Harper was embarrassed by her open evaluation. Harper wasn't exactly the self-conscious type herself, but it was different when Lauren was watching her.

"Nope, just Sal's hired help," Harper joked uneasily. Her eyes darted toward Lauren again. Lauren had turned in her chair to watch the exchange. She was smiling at Harper, but the expression didn't quite reach her eyes.

Martha gave her a wave. "It's nice to meet you. And seriously, you're gorgeous. I wish you were in the film. I'd love to paint that face of yours. It would be like working on a classic movie star."

"It's nice to meet you too," Harper said, ignoring the rest of her statement. Harper never gave that much thought to her looks and had always been confident enough, but Martha was definitely overdoing it.

Martha had gone back over to stand next to Lauren. "Don't you think she's gorgeous?" she asked, elbowing Lauren lightly and gesturing toward Harper.

Harper stood uncomfortably. Lauren was staring at her and wasn't smiling any more. Harper couldn't understand why Lauren didn't say anything. In any other circumstances, or if this exchange had occurred when they had first met, she might have assumed that Lauren was jealous of the attention. Harper knew now that Lauren wasn't like that, so her silence was puzzling.

Finally, Lauren looked back at the mirror. "Martha, we should get this done. I'm going to try to learn these as much as I can while you're working."

"I'd better be getting back to it too. Good luck with the new lines," Harper said, relieved that she'd been released from the conversation.

As soon as Harper had left the trailer, Martha resumed her work on Lauren's makeup.

"She really does look like she's from another time doesn't she? If I liked the ladies, I'd be all over that. Hell, maybe I would do it anyway if given the chance," Martha cackled.

"Do you have your next job booked already?" Lauren asked abruptly.

Lauren was desperate to change the subject, but thankfully Martha seemed to have no idea how uncomfortable the conversation was making her. Lauren knew she was expected to join in and that talking about another woman's looks was supposed to be no big deal, but she could never talk about Harper that way. She would mean it far too much. When Martha began talking about Harper's looks, Lauren just felt panicked.

Words that she shouldn't say had been on the tip of her tongue. That Harper was all the things Martha had said and more, and that she couldn't think of a more beautiful person.

The fact that Harper seemed so comfortable with herself only made her more attractive. Lauren didn't know if she was envious of Harper right now or just admired her. The dominant emotion was definitely admiration. Lauren just could not imagine being able to talk about her sexuality to colleagues as openly as Harper did. Harper's casual coming-out made her feel even more inauthentic.

Harper pointing out that she wasn't into guys had taken Lauren's breath away for other reasons. Harper was gay, and that meant there was a chance. Lauren's attraction to her had grown and had become more intense. It would be simpler if Harper were straight and unattainable. Not that Lauren thought a girl like Harper would necessarily be into her, but the revelation at least placed mutual feelings in the realm of possibility.

Lauren had found herself spending time lately wondering if Harper was in a relationship. And if she was, what did her partner look like? Was she pretty, or athletic, or really smart? Lauren would love to ask Harper if she had someone, but couldn't think of a way to do it that wouldn't make her sound nosy or inappropriate. They didn't know one another well enough yet. Yet Lauren was jealous of the hypothetical person she imagined, the one that might get to share a life with Harper.

Lauren tried to turn her thoughts away and focus on what Martha was saying, but her mind was a million miles away. It had followed Harper out of the door.

CHAPTER SEVEN

Since she had encountered Harper, Lauren had started walking around the same park each time she went out. It had tree-lined paths and a beautiful stone sculpture in the center, so it didn't bother her to keep coming back on the chance that she might run into Harper again. Though she barely knew Harper, talking to her made Lauren feel less alone. The town was full of strangers who were happy to say hello to her, but it was only when she talked to Harper that she felt fully seen. Harper had a gift for making her feel at ease, or at least that would be the case if Lauren weren't always so distracted by how attractive she was.

The fourth time Lauren returned to the park, she got her wish. She had taken Chester off his lead and was watching him run happily around in circles, his tongue hanging from his mouth. When she saw Harper jogging in their direction, she felt a surge of anxiety. It was always safer for her to imagine things in her own head than to have them actually happen no matter how much she wanted them to.

"Hi," Lauren greeted her. Harper looked impossibly attractive in her running clothes, a loose long shirt and tights that showed how toned her legs were.

"Hey!" Harper smiled back at her. "How are you? And how are you, little guy?"

She bent down and scratched Chester behind the ears. He had run over to them when he saw that Lauren was talking to someone. Chester jumped up and put his paws on Harper's thighs, eagerly panting up at her.

"Get down Chester!"

"I don't mind. He's so sweet. This little guy is really making me wish I had one of my own."

"He likes you. He's a little lonely, actually," Lauren said, aware that she might be talking about herself.

After the initial burst of enjoying solitude, she had started to miss having someone to talk to when she went home at night. Maybe she had been lonely for years, but her hectic schedule and the time she spent with her friends had helped to cover it up. Lauren had been trying to ignore the empty feeling and make the most of the time by herself. She baked more food than she would ever be able to eat. She read books that previously lay unopened in her apartment for months. During one restless night, she even pulled out a notebook and started jotting down ideas for a plot outline. She had forgotten how good it felt to be creative, how much it made her feel like she was doing something inspiring and important.

"Why is he lonely?" Harper asked.

"I've just been working such long days. Normally I've got an assistant with me to help out if I can't give him enough attention, but she stayed back home this time. I know I sound like I'm talking about a baby. He's not that high maintenance, but he does like company."

"Can't you bring him to the set? I thought I'd seen him with you there before?"

"I did at first, but it's harder to do that when I'm filming, I can't supervise him enough. He ends up being cooped up and tearing the place apart. Sal would kill me if I kept him with me and he interrupted filming."

"I'd be happy to help you look after him at work," Harper offered.

"You don't have to do that. But thank you so much."

"No, really, I'd love to have him around. If Sal doesn't object, I can take him with me while I'm doing errands and stuff. Between us he'd get plenty of attention. He seems like a really well behaved dog," Harper said, the sincerity in her eyes clear. Lauren was just now noticing how deep and brown they were, and it was hard to not get distracted.

Lauren nodded. "That would be amazing." Aside from the benefits it would yield for Chester, she quickly calculated it would give her a reason to talk to Harper more often. "We could always try it and see if it works out. Or just try doing it a couple of days a week. Even that would make a big difference. If it's too much trouble you can stop the arrangement, no questions asked. Thank you so much for thinking of it."

"No problem. If you're not doing anything right now, do you want to walk with me for a while?"

The two of them walked around the park making small talk. If she was careful to not look into those eyes, she could almost act completely normal.

When Harper arrived at work the next day, Lauren was waiting outside of the office. She had the end of Chester's leash wrapped around her wrist, and she was holding a big plastic container. Even though Lauren was standing in the place that they had talked about at the time they had agreed upon, she looked jumpy. It was as though she didn't think she was supposed to be there.

There were so many people walking up and down the hall that Lauren didn't seem to notice Harper's presence. Harper took in the delicate cheekbones and the hair that fell from her ponytail around her face. She was wearing an oversized T-shirt that made her look even smaller standing there. There was something about Lauren's vulnerability that caused a rush of tenderness in Harper. She had an urge to walk up to her and reassure her, to tell her that everything was okay. Why did someone as amazing as Lauren seem so unsure of herself all of the time?

Harper shook the thought from her head. It was a silly thing for her to be even thinking about. Lauren was a movie star with a boyfriend. There wasn't any person less suitable for her to take an interest in. It was harmless if she didn't let it get the better of her. To be fair, she wasn't even sure if it were the beginnings of a crush or just protectiveness she felt.

"Good morning." Harper loved watching Lauren come alive when she said hello, her sad expression erased. A slow shy smile spread until it lit up her whole face. They stood facing one another for a moment until Harper finally pointed out the plastic container Lauren held. "What have you got there?"

"Huh?" Lauren said, looking down at her hands. "They're for you. As a thank you," she muttered, offering the container.

"That's so lovely of you. Thanks." Harper took the container from her and opened a corner of the lid. The smell of freshly baked muffins reached her nose.

"Double chocolate. I hope you like muffins?" Lauren said.

"You bet I do, especially chocolate. You really didn't have to, but thanks again."

Lauren pushed a piece of hair behind her ear and smiled at Harper. The smile was so warm and open and its loveliness struck Harper unexpectedly. Harper's stomach fluttered as she smiled back. One of the assistant director's voices interrupted them.

"You're needed in makeup." Lauren nodded and looked at Harper regretfully before trailing after him.

Now that the arrangement was in place, they settled into an easy routine with Chester. Lauren would drop him off in the mornings and pick him up as soon as she was finished working. During breaks she would drop in and take him for a while, but Harper didn't mind how often he was around. Chester was easy to look after and he fit in neatly around her work, as she had thought he would.

Harper liked seeing more of Lauren. Often she would stay for a while and they would talk about work and whatever was happening that day. Lauren seemed to be getting more comfortable around her, and was not quite as reticent. It fascinated Harper to see Lauren coming out of her shell, to hear her begin to tell sly jokes and give her opinions on things. Harper had a CD player in her office and Lauren knew and liked a lot of the songs that she played—so they would sit and talk about music, sparring happily about songs and genres. Lauren teased Harper about her affection for musical theater, telling her that she was nerdy because of her love for show tunes. They each liked punk music and Harper was impressed by Lauren's knowledge of the bands Harper was into. They agreed that Patti Smith was a genius and that more people should listen to The Modern Lovers.

They soon discovered that they both liked to read, and they started trading books back and forth. Harper tried to introduce Lauren to some of her favorite Southern writers but found that Lauren was already familiar with most of them. They discovered a mutual love of Carson McCullers. Lauren promised to have an autobiography she owned sent down from home so that Harper could borrow it. Neither of them tried to shift the conversation to more intimate matters, but Harper still felt that she was getting to know Lauren.

One Friday afternoon there was a knocking on Harper's door, and Lauren poked her head in to the office.

"Hey," Lauren said, waving at her. Harper stopped typing, noticing how un-self-consciously Lauren stepped inside. "Where's Chester?"

"Hey you. He's under the desk. Pretty sure he's asleep." Harper smiled at the comfortable sensation of fur brushing against her ankles and a heavy little body on her feet.

"No problem. If you could just kick him until he wakes up that would be great," Lauren deadpanned.

"I'm really going to have to report you to animal rescue one of these days soon." Harper gently picked Chester up and felt him wake up against her hands. Harper's heart rate began to accelerate as Lauren leaned toward her to take him. She watched Lauren walk toward the door with the dog in her arms, her eyes dropping to see the way she moved in her jeans.

"Hey, um…" Lauren was standing in the doorway, clutching Chester. "Seeing as it looks like we're going to get an early finish, a few of us are going to get a drink tonight. Would you like to come?"

"Sure." For the past two weeks, it had been on the tip of her tongue to ask Lauren out for a coffee or a drink, but she hadn't summoned up the courage yet. It wasn't like her to be so slow about making an invitation. With Lauren, it felt important to be the one who was receiving it. "Where are you going?"

"The Tavern, at six o'clock. I'm going to do a few things at home, like dropping this one off, and then I'll be there."

"Sounds great. I'll see you there," Harper said.

"Great." Lauren took Chester's paws between her fingers and used it to wave good-bye. Harper grinned and waved back.

When Harper entered the bar, a number of people she recognized were already sitting around a table. Harper gave a wave, feeling like she was in the cafeteria on her first day of school. With relief she saw there was an empty seat next to Lauren, who beckoned her over. The makeup artist she'd already met, Martha, greeted Harper warmly when she sat down.

Lauren was wearing a simple black top and dark blue jeans. It was how Harper liked to see her best, looking comfortable and at ease in her skin. Lauren had told her that she hated getting dressed up for events in designer clothes, that it made her feel like a glorified coat hanger.

Harper couldn't remember the last time she had gone out to a bar. It might have been years. She and her friends from the diner would get together now and then for a barbecue or one of their kids' birthday parties, but they didn't go out on the town. When she was younger and home on trips from college she went to The Tavern regularly, because everyone went there and there would always be someone to hang out with. It had a jukebox and notoriously sticky floors, and more different types of liquor than one would imagine in such a small-town place.

Lauren was drinking beer, so Harper bought them a pitcher to share. She almost never drank these days so the alcohol hit her fast, spreading a feeling of warmth and goodwill through her. Harper looked around at the faces at the table, taking in the strange reality that she found herself in the middle of. There were actors and a director and members of the crew, people she could never have imagined meeting. Martha was regaling her with tales of diva stars that she had worked with over the years, making Harper laugh.

Still, Harper's attention was focused on Lauren, who she could see in her peripheral vision. Now and then she felt Lauren glancing over at her and Martha. She wondered hopefully if Lauren might be looking for a chance to speak to her as well.

When Martha got up to go and get a drink, Harper turned to Lauren with a question on her lips. Lauren had turned to her at the same moment, and they smiled at one another. A ripple of excitement ran through Harper.

"I just realized I've never actually asked you where you're staying in town," she said "Are you at the Regent?"

As far as she knew, most of the cast and crew were staying there. It was the only nice hotel around, a hundred-year-old building that had been lovingly renovated.

"No, I've got a rental down on Walker Street," said Lauren. "I like to get a homey place when I can. Makes me feel more settled, and it's much better for Chester too. There's a little yard for him to run around in."

"Some nice places on Walker. Is Josh staying there too?" Harper asked. Lauren never mentioned Josh when they talked. It made her wonder if the tabloid stories about trouble between them might be true. A surge of irrational jealousy coursed through her when she thought about Lauren with Josh, a feeling that she would be mortified about if anyone else ever noticed it. However, if she and Lauren were going to be friendly with one another, she had to ask the kind of questions that a friend would ask.

Lauren frowned, her eyes narrowing in confusion. "With Josh? Why would he live with me?"

"Aren't you two...?" Harper said. She was sorry that she had raised the issue. She shook her head, wishing she could take it back. Was it common knowledge that they had broken up? She watched a range of expressions quickly pass over Lauren's face, and she had no idea what they meant. "I'm sorry, I just thought that..."

Lauren put a hand on her shoulder for a moment. "It's okay. But we're not together." The way she said it was kind but firm, and it left no room for further questions.

Harper apologized again. It was not the first time that her curiosity had gotten her into trouble. She had a tendency to ask questions that people didn't like. Sometimes she envied people like Lauren for how reserved they were.

"So, what about you?" Lauren asked, looking into her drink when she spoke. "Do you have a girlfriend?"

"Not at the moment, no. Not exactly a huge dating pool for me in this town," Harper looked around at the other bar patrons and raised her eyebrows. Aside from the people in their party, they were surrounded by either guys over the age of fifty, or people who looked like they had barely reached legal drinking age. They looked at one another solemnly and then Lauren laughed. Harper realized that she had developed a habit of trying to get that reaction. Harper loved making Lauren loosen up, loved to know that Lauren was happy, and she especially loved knowing that she was the cause of it.

Lauren bought them another pitcher. Harper watched her fingers when she wiped condensation from the side of her glass, then followed them as they fiddled with a napkin on the table.

"So where do you live usually?" Harper asked her. "In LA, like Sal?"

"No way. New York. I have an apartment in the East Village."

"Really?" Harper asked, memories flooding back to her. "I can't believe we haven't talked about this before, we would have found out that I'm a bit of a New Yorker myself. I lived there for a few years."

They talked about the city and everything they loved and hated about it. They had hung out at some of the same places, had neighborhoods and streets they knew in common.

"I used to go to this crappy bar called Manny's all the time," said Harper. "They knew me so well. I practically lived there. They did coffee and late night breakfasts and things too, so I'd go there in the middle of the night."

Lauren's face lit up as soon as she said the name. She leaned forward eagerly. "I know that place! I'm convinced they do the best pizza in the whole city, and trust me I've gone everywhere."

"They do! Do you know Nina?"

"Do I? I'm pretty sure she's the coolest person I've ever met. Did you know she's the one who picks out all the music they play there?"

"Yep. I used to ask her to make me CDs, and she'd do it, told me I needed the education. I still have them actually. Man, I'd love to go back there one day."

The rest of their party was starting to slowly peel away, coming over one by one to say goodnight. Harper knew she should make a move to go home, but she didn't want to stop spending time with Lauren. Tomorrow's hangover felt so far away, and there was a magical feeling about tonight that she wanted to hold on to. She loved the closeness they were sharing, the way that any awkwardness that had existed between them had vanished. It wasn't just the alcohol, because the beer had only given them an excuse to talk more.

After a few more minutes, Harper became aware that it was closing time. She turned around and saw chairs being placed onto tables, weary-looking staff looking pleased to be wrapping up for the night.

"If you're on Walker Street you're on my way home. I'll walk you back. I'll walk you to Walker Street," Harper rambled. Lauren happily agreed.

It was balmy outside, the sort of night Harper loved. The streets were eerily quiet, but she had always felt safe in her town, especially now that she wasn't on her own. To her surprise, Lauren linked an arm through hers as they walked. They each fell silent. Harper could feel warm, soft skin against her as they brushed up against one another.

"I'm cold," Lauren said. It was impossible to be cold in this weather but Harper took her at her word, running a hand over Lauren's forearm to warm her. She felt goose flesh under her fingers and wondered if maybe Lauren really was freezing, or at least scared of the empty streets. Harper liked protecting Lauren, making her feel safe and warm.

When they reached Lauren's cottage, they stopped at the front. Lauren extricated her arm, coughing as though to cover discomfort when she slid it out from Harper's light grasp. Harper looked at the house hulking in the dark, its face illuminated by the porch light.

"This place is beautiful," Harper said. Her gaze fell on Lauren, who stared back at her. Though she knew that the connection she was making with Lauren was platonic, she had the same sensation she might have after a successful first date. Right now felt like the moment when she was supposed to walk Lauren up to that light and kiss her beneath it. Lauren's lips looked like they would be soft. She longed to taste them. Harper wondered what kind of kisser Lauren would be. Would she let Harper push her up against the door like she wanted to? Would she be passionate or would she hold back?

The thought was ridiculous. It had been too long since Harper had kissed a woman, and she must be more intoxicated than she had realized.

"Thanks for walking me home. Are you sure it's safe for you to go on by yourself?"

Harper nodded. "It'll only take me a little while and the way's well lit. Thanks for inviting me along tonight. I had fun."

"Me too." Lauren was playing with the keys in her hand and had made no move to leave Harper's side. "Are you doing much tomorrow?"

"You mean aside from sleeping in? Not really, no plans," Harper said. If only Lauren knew how boring her life was. Saturdays were usually spent doing chores around the house and reading.

"Would you like to come over to dinner? As a thank-you for everything you've been doing for Chester? I'd like to show you around the place properly too." Lauren was doing that cute nervous thing where she shifted from foot to foot.

"You've already thanked me plenty, Lauren."

Lauren looked disappointed. "Okay, well if you're busy…"

Harper shook her head. "No, I'd love to come around, I just don't want you to think you have to have me."

Lauren smiled at her again, looking endearingly shy and pleased with herself. "That's settled then. Come around at seven? You know where I live," she said, pointing with a thumb behind her.

"I'll be here," Harper agreed and watched as Lauren opened the door and disappeared inside. After a beat Harper finally walked on, feeling keenly aware of the empty space beside her.

CHAPTER EIGHT

When Lauren woke up the next morning, she felt tingles of anticipation mixed in with fear. It had not been part of the plan to invite Harper over for dinner. It wasn't that she regretted it, at least not now that Harper had actually said yes, but she wished that she had more time to prepare. She also hoped she wasn't coming across as overly eager for wanting to spend time with Harper two nights in a row.

The memory of Harper's face came back to her, gorgeous in the semidarkness. Lauren had wanted to kiss her so badly that in that instant she hadn't cared about anything else. She had forgotten all of the reasons why she shouldn't. When Harper touched her arm, she felt desire that was disproportionate to the gesture. It was the type of longing that made the thought of spending two days away from Harper impossible to manage. All she wanted was to do something to extend her good fortune, because she couldn't believe how well the night had gone. Their conversations had always been enjoyable but superficial, and last night they had started to really get to know one another.

Lauren began preparations for the meal and cleaned the cottage from top to bottom. It helped to ease her hangover to drive out of town to a farmer' market and then spend the afternoon drinking coffee and chopping vegetables. Normally if she were having a dinner party, it would be a big production with a lot of people buzzing around her house. It was nice to do this all by herself.

As seven o'clock approached, Lauren's restlessness increased. She couldn't sit still, and when she tried to her leg jogged up and down. The doorbell rang at last and Lauren buzzed with happiness at the sight of Harper, standing there shaking the water from her umbrella. She was stunning.

"It's raining cats and dogs out here!" Harper said as she stepped through the door. Shyness made Lauren pause for a moment before she could move forward to help Harper with the light coat she was wearing to protect her from the rain. When Lauren took the coat, she noticed the racing of her own heart.

"I'm sorry, I hope I don't get water all over your house," Harper said, looking down at the damp bottoms of her jeans.

"Don't worry, it's fine. Should I give you the tour?" Lauren asked.

Harper nodded and ran a hand through her wet hair. As they looked around the cottage, she exclaimed over how nice everything was. Chester followed the two of them as they walked from room to room.

"This place is really special," Harper said.

"Isn't it? I wish I could have it picked up and dropped off in New York. It makes me so happy to be here."

"I can see why. What is that delicious smell?" Harper asked as they made their way to the kitchen.

"Roast lamb. I hope you like garlic?"

"I love it."

They took a seat at the dining table and Lauren served out the meal. Lauren watched apprehensively while Harper bit into the meat. Harper closed her eyes as she chewed and lightly slapped her hand on the table. "Holy shit. You can cook! Now that I know this I'll be expecting you to cook for me more often."

"I'll do it gladly."

"Who taught you?"

"Nobody. Trial and error mainly. I mangled a lot of food before I got the hang of it. You wouldn't want to get near any of my early attempts."

"Practice makes perfect then, because this is delicious. I like the rosemary."

"It came out of the garden. Can I get you some wine?" Lauren went to the rack that lined the dining room wall. "The landlady said I could open something from the collection, she's been super generous." Lauren chose a bottle of red that she knew would match well and poured them each a glass.

"What is this magic dream house? You know how to enjoy yourself. There's nothing better than good food and good wine. I mean it, we should do this more often. If you don't mind me inviting myself around, that is."

Lauren held up her glass. "Let's seal that with a toast. And when we're done, shall we retire to the living room? I made a blueberry pie if you want some."

"That would be perfect."

They curled up before the fireplace in the ancient armchairs, and Lauren brought the pie and ice cream in from the kitchen. Because it was unseasonably cool, the heat breaking with a summer storm, she had lit a fire. Lauren felt lazy and content, like she could sit here all night listening to the crackling of the fire and the sound of the rain outside.

Harper looked just as content as she ate her pie. Lauren bit her lip while she watched Harper's mouth. Her eyes were drawn to Harper's tongue as it darted out to lick away stray crumbs from the corner of her mouth. Harper had a way of showing how much pleasure she took in eating, her full lips closing around each bite as though she couldn't get enough of the flavors. Lauren was warm at having elicited that reaction.

They were quiet for a moment, both of them staring at the fireplace.

"Penny for your thoughts?" Harper asked.

"I don't feel like I'm doing what I'm supposed to be doing with my life," Lauren said. It was the first thought she could pluck from her brain, the first one that didn't pertain to Harper or how attractive she was. Besides, the fire was making her reflective.

Harper blinked at her and then smiled. "Okay, you don't mess around. Starting off deep."

Lauren shook her head, laughing at herself. "I've never been that great at small talk."

"No, it's okay. I like that. And I mean, I can relate. Tell me what you want to be doing."

How could Lauren explain, knowing how ridiculous she must sound? She was aware that a lot of people wanted a life like the one she had. She had wanted it too, once, and she had worked hard to get where she was now. Feeling ungrateful for her success was part of the reason why she felt so guilty most of the time. It wasn't fair that she had so much money, more than any one person had a right to have, and she couldn't even appreciate it. She didn't do anything to earn it, not really. There were people so much more deserving than she was.

The last time she had felt truly fulfilled by work was when she was doing *Edge of the Sea*. When she had written that script, she wasn't famous like she was now. She was practically an unknown back then, and there wasn't the sense that anyone was watching her or that there was anything to lose. Now her situation was very different, and people would love to tear her to pieces. Nobody thought of her as a writer. She knew how people would react if she tried something and it didn't work out. But she wished she had the confidence to try.

"It's nothing important," Lauren said finally. "I just sometimes feel like I'm wasting my time with these movies. I'm just helping add more mindless garbage to the world."

Harper sipped from her mug. "I don't mean to dismiss the way you're feeling. I'm not going to act as though I think movies like *Texas Twist* are fine art, but I don't think they're a waste either."

"I don't mean to sound snobby. I know Sal's talented and that a lot of people like romantic stuff. I just can't really relate to it myself," Lauren explained.

"Me neither, if I'm honest. But you have to admit they make a lot of people happy. Who are we to say what's worthwhile and what's not, if people get pleasure from them? People want to think about love being real. That's worth making movies about."

"But it's never simple in real life though. These movies don't represent anything like what love actually is."

"Maybe not. But you've only got ninety minutes or so to tell a story, so some things just aren't going to make that final cut," Harper said. "It's not really supposed to be real life, is it? Nobody would watch that."

"You make a good point." She had quickly come to trust Harper's opinion, and liked the way she was able to cast things in a different light.

"Yep. And besides, in my experience, love can be simple. Maybe not like in the movies, but still. Nobody teaches us or tells us whom to love. It just finds you."

Lauren wasn't aware of having any expression at all on her face, but she knew that she must have given herself away when Harper looked concerned. "I'm sorry, did I say something wrong?"

Lauren tried to brighten. "Of course not. It's just never found me, that's all. I've never really been in love."

Lauren tried to say it like it was no big deal, like it was just another fact about herself. The truth was that she had never said that out loud to anyone, never quite admitted to love's absence even to people who knew her well. It had always felt more important to her to act experienced and on top of everything. In some ways she *was* experienced, but the relationships that she'd had never seemed to really touch her. There was always a distance between her and the women she dated. It would be easy to blame it on the constraints she lived with because of her work, but that wasn't the only reason. She worried that the problem was with her. She had always been afraid that there was something about her that made her incapable of sustaining a relationship.

Lauren felt like she could tell Harper the whole story of her life and be understood. She could tell her about the constant moving from place to place. The parents who had walked in and out of her life, leaving her with whichever relatives were willing to take her at the time. Harper might be willing to listen to the way it had made her feel like she was never on solid ground. She had always been a guest in this place or that and never really felt accepted anywhere. Maybe Harper would understand why Lauren had found it so hard to trust people even before her most recent mistakes. Maybe Lauren could even tell Harper about Angela.

Yet the last thing she wanted was for Harper to think of her as messed up, or as a person that she should feel sorry for. She had spent her whole life trying to outrun such assumptions and attitudes. Lauren stayed silent.

"Never?" Harper asked, and Lauren was relieved that she could detect nothing pitying in her tone. When Lauren shook her head, Harper reached over and grasped her fingers just for a second. "You will, if that's what you want."

Lauren's stomach fluttered, and she took a calming sip from her mug. She'd wanted to grab Harper's fingers and not let them go. "What about you?"

"Sure, I've been there once or twice. Nothing earth-shattering, but I had a good thing going on for a couple of years once."

"Oh, sorry." Lauren ducked her head, realizing that she had been misunderstood. "I meant to ask about work. You said you could relate before to how I was feeling."

Harper laughed. "Oh, I see. Yes, I can relate. Technically I'm a lawyer, but I haven't worked as one since I came back home a couple of years ago. So that's what I feel like I should be doing."

"You're a lawyer?"

"I guess I don't really think of myself as that anymore. I came home a few years ago for a bunch of reasons and my career stalled. I keep thinking I'll go back to it one day, but I'm not sure."

Lauren thought she detected something of her own wistfulness in Harper's tone. It seemed there were decisions that they both regretted, lives that they had both wanted to lead and didn't have the strength or the courage to follow through on. It made her feel closer to Harper.

They talked into the night. It was difficult for Lauren to imagine that they would ever run out of subjects to discuss, because their words ran swiftly from one topic to the next. Their dialogue switched back and forth between the deep and the trivial, but Lauren never felt bored by it. Every now and then she would get up to make them another hot drink. The first time she did it, she took a moment in the kitchen to marvel that this was all going so wonderfully. It was even better than the night before had been, because they were really alone and there was no alcohol or distractions.

They were talking about a writer they both admired, and whom Lauren had been lucky enough to meet, when Harper glanced at the clock on the wall. "Wow, it's really late. I should probably be getting going."

"I can drive you home. I only had that one glass of wine over dinner."

"Thank you, it would be great to not have to walk back in this weather."

The rain had been steadily falling outside, punctuated by the occasional clap of thunder. Lauren had always loved these types of storms—she had been able to smell this one coming in the air all day. She watched while Harper stretched and yawned, her back arching and her chest moving forward. Lauren swallowed hard as she watched the movement and had to force her eyes away. Lauren didn't actually want to take Harper home, and she had the sense that Harper didn't really want to go either. She wished she had the nerve to ask her to stay.

As soon as they opened the door, Lauren realized how much worse the weather was than she had thought. The driveway was flooded and the rain was coming down in thick sheets. A burst of lightning came, beautiful forks of it running over the black sky. There was a second when it was as bright as midday.

Lauren could swear for a moment she felt something between them, a leaping toward one another. She wanted to reach out and put her hand on Harper's shoulder and slide it through her hair.

Finally, Harper broke the silence. "I can't let you drive in this! Maybe I should call my dad, see if he can pick me up..." she said doubtfully.

Lauren stepped back into the hall, holding the door open and beckoning Harper inside. "It's so late and your dad's not going to find it any easier to drive in this than I would. Why don't you just stay here?"

"Thanks, but I'll figure something out. I don't want to impose."

"Don't be silly. You won't be. You're more than welcome," Lauren said, forcing herself to sound light and breezy.

When Harper agreed, Lauren went into motion, focusing on the practical tasks that needed to be done so she wouldn't have to think too much. She went to the bedroom, rifling through her drawers until she found a long shirt that Harper could sleep in. She walked back out to the living room with the shirt and her own pajamas. She was awkwardly carrying a spare blanket and pillow under her arm, and she dropped them onto the sofa. When she was done, she held out the shirt to Harper.

"Here. You can sleep in this. There's a bathroom off my room, you'll find a new toothbrush in the top drawer. I'll sleep out here," Lauren said in a rush. It was doubtful that she would be able to sleep, even considering how tired she was—not with the awareness of the fact that Harper was lying in the next room. Harper looked between the sofa and Lauren.

"I don't really like the idea of pushing you out of your bed," Harper said.

"It's fine. I don't mind."

"I should take it."

Lauren shook her head. "No, please." She didn't mind her own discomfort, but she knew very well that the short sofa was too small for either of them. She would have to sleep in a very awkward position.

"C'mon, we'll both sleep in the bed. You don't have a single bed, do you?" Harper called out, already walking into the bedroom.

Lauren didn't reply. Harper would see for herself that her bed was more than big enough for two. It had been one of the many selling points of this cottage, the big, pillowy, king-sized bed. She could just get on the sofa and not follow Harper into the bedroom, because any further insistence on Harper's part would be strange. However, friends slept in the same bed together all of the time, and she didn't want to make an issue out of it. Harper obviously felt comfortable in her company and didn't think it was a big deal to share a bed, so neither should she.

She knew she was going to do what Harper was asking her to because she wanted to. It was pathetic, but she loved the idea of being in the same bed with Harper, of sleeping next to her and being so close.

Lauren moved into the main bathroom and prepared for bed. She took her time over cleaning her teeth and washing her face, hoping that Harper would already be asleep by the time she was done. When she tiptoed into the bedroom, she saw Harper's form curled over onto her side. The room was dark save for the light of the lamp on her nightstand. Lauren crawled into the bed gingerly, trying to not disturb Harper, then rolled over and turned off her lamp. The click was painfully loud and she braced, wondering if Harper would stir.

It was sweet torture, the way she felt. She could roll over and touch her, if only Harper wanted her to. It couldn't be true, it must only be wishful thinking, but she had felt intimacy between them tonight that made the thought seem not so crazy. Even if she were right Lauren knew she could never act upon her feelings. What kind of a person would she be if she couldn't stick to her resolve to avoid attachments for even a couple of months? After Angela, she was supposed to be keeping to herself.

Lauren closed her eyes and tried to relax. Despite the tension that arose from being in this situation, she was weary. A sudden jolt of fear raced through her and she jumped like she'd had a falling dream, the kind that came upon her when she was closest to sleep. In her half-awake state it had occurred to her that someone might have seen Harper come into her house and never leave it.

If someone wanted to dig around, they might find out about Harper's sexuality. She was so open about it that anyone could find out if they asked questions of the right people. Just because Lauren hadn't seen the paparazzi yet didn't mean that there wasn't one or two in the area, just waiting to catch her at something. It wouldn't be the first time that they had sought her out with long lenses. She had long ago learned that they were willing to go to any lengths for a shot they could sell. The fact that she and Harper hadn't actually done anything meant nothing, they only needed a grain of truth and they could fabricate the rest.

When she jumped, she felt Harper put a hand out. It came to rest on her thigh over the sheet for a moment. Lauren was desperate to touch Harper, need threatening to overcome her. It was worse when Harper took her hand away and she became sure that it had only been an unconscious gesture.

Lauren folded herself up carefully to make sure she wasn't close to Harper's side of the bed. Yet, when she closed her eyes, Harper was all that she thought of.

CHAPTER NINE

The birds were singing outside when Harper woke up. The curtains were heavy enough that she could only see light where it bordered the thick material. They hadn't been long in bed, but the need to go to the bathroom pressed her awake. She figured she could get to the en suite without waking Lauren if she were quiet. Then she could come back to bed. It was unbelievably cozy, and she wanted to stay for as long as she could.

As she rolled out of bed and her feet landed softly on the thick carpet, she looked over her shoulder. Lauren was lying on her back with an arm flung over her head. The sheet covered her up to the waist. Harper guiltily noted the thinness of her tank top, the lines of Lauren's beautiful body clear. What struck her most however, was the peaceful expression on Lauren's face. She knew by now that Lauren wasn't a grumpy person and that she had a great sense of humor. Still there was a subtle darkness to her most of the time. Lauren always looked like she was thinking about something important. Her features were always just an inch away from a frown.

Not now. Now she looked relaxed and almost blissful. Harper sat for a moment watching her, the beauty enough to astound her.

Harper crept to the bathroom and then back again. Before getting into the bed she picked up the glass of water Lauren had thoughtfully placed there and took a long drink. When she glanced back over again, she saw that Lauren's eyes were wide open.

The room was darkened but not so much that Lauren wouldn't be able to see that she was standing there in nothing but a shirt and underwear. Harper was taller than Lauren, so the shirt didn't cover her up all that much. She felt almost naked under Lauren's gaze. She had a crazy urge to pull her shirt over her head, to reveal herself. It felt too still to speak or apologize so Harper got back into bed and lay on her side. As she felt Lauren's heat beside her, her breath quickened. She slowed it down deliberately.

It was much later when she woke up again, and this time she was alone. She sat up, looked at the digital clock on the nightstand, and saw it was already nine. Harper put out her hand and could feel that the bed was still warm. Lauren must not have been up for long.

Harper yawned and went into the en suite to get dressed in yesterday's clothes. As she neared the kitchen, she could smell coffee brewing. Harper stood in the doorway and watched Lauren for just a moment. Her face was scrubbed clean of makeup and her hair was tied carelessly back, with dark strands framing her face. Lauren was barefoot and was still in her tank top and some comfortable-looking shorts. The sight of her bare legs shot through Harper; she wished she could touch Lauren's skin. From where she was standing Harper could only see her profile, but there was enough of her face visible that Harper could see that she was frowning. Harper wanted badly to put her arms around her, to smooth that brow again.

"Good morning," Harper said.

Lauren jumped as though caught at something, and then she smiled. "Sorry. Can I get you a coffee?"

Harper accepted gratefully. Her eyes were bleary and tired, not having slept much at all over the past couple of nights. She sipped her coffee, and they stood in silence. Lauren was drinking her coffee while she leaned up against the countertop, jogging her leg up and down. Harper wanted to still it with her hand, but didn't know that the touch would be welcome. Harper had a suspicion that if she didn't offer to leave Lauren would come up with some reason why she needed to go out. She wasn't sure why things were so awkward this morning. That moment between them in the dawn felt ridiculously charged to her, but nothing had actually happened. Maybe Lauren was just tired.

Despite the unease she felt in their good-byes there was a spring in Harper's step as she walked home. The last couple of days, spending so much time with Lauren, had been wonderful. It brought the loneliness of her life into stark focus. Lauren kept surprising her with the quiet way she had of being kind and compassionate.

It had been interesting to hear Lauren say that she had never been in love. The relationship with Josh must have ended badly or must not have been very deep. Harper had always thought there was nothing wrong with being single. She also believed that the pressure society placed on people to be coupled up was ridiculous. Still, everyone deserved to feel love, and she could see that it upset Lauren. Her eyes were so sad when she talked about that.

It was clear that Lauren had gone to a lot of trouble over cooking dinner for the two of them. Everything was made from scratch and was delicious. Harper would love to return the favor and invite Lauren over for a Southern home cooked meal, but they weren't the sort of family who entertained very often. In fact, she didn't think they'd had anyone over to dinner since her mother died. It had been a while since she wished she had her own place, as she just wasn't ready for Lauren to meet her family. There was so much sadness in her home. The memory of her mother's death lingered in every square inch of it.

In a flash of inspiration, she realized that she could invite Lauren out to a picnic. That way she could still cook, but she wouldn't have to worry about all the stress associated with having Lauren over.

"Hey, Dad," she said, walking into the kitchen at home.

"Where have you been young lady?" he asked, tongue-in-cheek, scraping eggs onto his plate.

"I stayed at Lauren's place. It was too miserable out to get back."

"I gathered. Am I going to get to meet this new gal of yours?"

"Dad, she's just a friend."

"Oh, right. Whatever you say."

He sat down at the kitchen table and started shoveling eggs into his mouth. His red-rimmed eyes made Harper wonder when he'd gotten to bed the night before. When he picked up his coffee mug, Harper could smell the whiskey in it even from where she was sitting.

"This so-called friend of yours, maybe I could meet her sometime?"

"Maybe. Maybe I'll invite her around when you finally shave, how does that sound?" Harper said.

He rubbed his stubble and narrowed his eyes at her. "Don't try to change the subject, girly. How'd you like it if I told you when to shave your legs?"

"I take your point. As for Lauren coming over, we'll see."

Harper rose and started to clean up the pile of dishes sitting by the sink. She had no intention of changing her mind, not with her dad making insinuations. Once he got something into his head, it was impossible to convince him of the truth.

Lauren was delivering Chester to her when Harper asked her on the picnic. Lauren hesitated at first, then seemed to change her mind and gave Harper a satisfyingly firm yes. Harper suggested they go for a drive to a place just out of town. There was a beautiful spot by the lake that was perfect, a clearing that Harper went to sometimes to read and take time out for herself. No matter what was going on in her life, she always felt better when she came back from there.

When the weekend arrived, Harper packed a basket full of cucumber sandwiches, a salad, fruit, iced tea, beer and an apple pie that she'd baked. Mother Nature co-operated by giving them perfect weather to enjoy. It was sunny, but not too hot. As Harper drove them, she looked over and saw Lauren gazing out the window at the passing trees, a secret smile on her lips. This place was special, especially when you were used to being in New York, where scenes like these were hard to come by.

They laid out a blanket and sat looking out over the lake. Chester chased birds around the water's edge. Harper had brought a portable CD player, and Billie Holiday sang a slow, lazy tune in the background.

"I am so relaxed right now," Lauren said, sighing. "Sometimes I think I could live in this town. It's so quiet, like everything's slowed down."

"You wouldn't miss the Big Apple?" Harper teased. "I know I did, when I moved back here."

"Of course I would. I can't believe you used to live there. I wonder if we ever passed one another in the street. Or if we were at Manny's on the same nights. Wouldn't it be funny if we were?"

"I think I'd remember you," Harper said, the words slipping from her lips before she had a chance to think about them. It sounded embarrassingly suggestive. Harper avoided Lauren's eyes, glancing down at her legs instead. They were perfectly toned and smooth. Lauren had shown up for the picnic in a casual summer dress, looking so cute it gave Harper butterflies.

"If you missed it, does that mean you didn't really want to come back to Texas?" Lauren finally asked.

"Not really." Harper fiddled with a piece of grass, wondering how much to share. She got the sense Lauren had picked up on her vagueness, and was aware that she had been evasive when they spoke about this before. After considering it for a few moments, she was sure that she didn't have to worry about talking to Lauren. Although they had only just started to get to know one another, it was obvious that Lauren was a sensitive person.

"I came back because my mom got diagnosed with cancer. We really thought she was going to get better—hoped so anyway. She died a couple of years ago."

"I'm so sorry."

"Thanks."

"What was she like?"

"She was great. I mean, we had our differences but she was a great mom and we were close. We got even closer before the end."

"That all must have been so hard, on the whole family."

"It was. Tommy's still so young, and Dad kind of lost it. He started drinking, stopped working. That's why I've stayed. It feels like everyone's still stuck back there, like everyone's scared that if we move on it'll mean we have to deal with her really being gone. Everyone's done their best I guess, but I've had to take a lot on."

Lauren scooted closer to her and took Harper's hand in her own. They stared out at the water with their fingers laced together. There was nothing that Harper wanted Lauren to say, because she could feel how much she cared.

"It's funny, everyone in town knew her," Harper continued. "They all brought meals and stuff to the house after, and I don't think there's anyone in the community who didn't come to her funeral."

"It sounds like everyone loved her."

"They did, but that's not what I meant. I think this is the first time I've told anyone about it since she died. Everyone already knows. This is new for me. Do you know what I mean?"

Lauren squeezed her hand. "Thank you for telling me."

They were talking about the saddest memories of her life, but some of the pain fell away in the wake of Lauren's touch. The hurt would never leave her, but with the passage of time it had dulled to a manageable ache. With the feel of Lauren's skin against her own, she had the sensation more than ever that everything was going to be okay. There was a solidity to Lauren, a presence that reassured Harper that she wasn't alone in the world.

"I know that we don't know one another very well, but I'm really glad we met," Harper said, opening her eyes. Lauren was looking at her mouth, and she could swear that she could feel Lauren's fingers trembling where they were joined.

"I am too," Lauren replied.

To Harper it looked like she was trying to compose her thoughts, like words were being shaped in her mouth and then discarded. Harper wished she could lean over and kiss that mouth, to fully take comfort from Lauren in the way that she wanted. She felt consumed by phantom sensations, sure of how soft and warm Lauren's lips must be. At that moment, Chester ran up and jumped onto her lap. Harper's hand was empty now, so she closed her fingers and put her hand in her lap. She watched Lauren ruffle Chester's fur, feeling like she had dodged a bullet because she hadn't given into her impulses.

"I feel like I shouldn't complain about it, especially after you've just told me what you've been through, but it's really hard to meet genuine people when you're in my position, you know?" Lauren said, scratching under Chester's chin. Harper watched the movement of her fingers. She wished she could pull the hand away, and bring it toward her.

"No, come on. I don't think like that. That actually sounds really lonely."

"It is. But it's been so great finding someone I can talk to."

There was a long pause, but Harper could see that Lauren wanted to say more, so she stayed quiet. It made her feel guilty that she had been sitting here thinking sexual thoughts when Lauren was talking about how important their friendship was to her. Harper knew that if she tried hard enough, she could hold both things inside of her at once. She could balance friendship and longing. Harper just needed to learn how to compartmentalize and to separate Lauren the friend from Lauren the woman she was starting to really want.

"Will you keep in touch with me when I'm gone?" Lauren continued. "I meet so many different people through work, and we always say we're going to see one another again, but we don't. We get close for a couple of months and then they just become an acquaintance, someone I see at events and used to know. I would hate for that to happen to us."

"I don't think I've ever heard you say so much at one time before. Anyways, I don't think I'm going to see you at the Oscars any time soon, so that definitely won't happen with us," Harper joked, pushing at Lauren with her elbow.

Lauren looked sideways at her, rolling her eyes and smiling in that dry way she had sometimes. "You know what I mean."

"Of course we can stay in touch. Maybe I can even visit you sometime. I never get back to the city anymore, even though I still have friends and my uncle there. It could give me a good excuse to actually go."

Lauren sounded earnest about staying in touch, but Harper wondered how much she would follow through. Lauren seemed unhappy with her life as it usually was now, but surely she would feel differently when she went back to New York. Harper had lived there herself, and she knew how quickly she had become accustomed to life there and how much it had started to feel like a chore to come back to this little place and visit. Harper was sure she was boring in comparison to Lauren's New York friends.

Then Lauren turned to her with such an expression of happiness and hope that Harper wondered if she was being unfair when she doubted her. "Would you really? I'd love to spend time in the city with you. I have a guest room in my apartment. You could stay as often as you wanted."

"I'd really like that," Harper said. She hadn't realized that Lauren considered her a good enough friend to invite to come to stay at her home, and the thought warmed her all over. "We could go to Manny's."

"Manny's is really all you care about, isn't it?" Lauren said, grinning slyly at her.

"Well, yes. I can't really get good pizza around here, you know."

"Then it's settled. You must come to New York on the pretext of seeing me, but mainly so that you can have some decent pie."

Harper laughed, lying back on the picnic blanket. The combination of the beer and the sun was making her sleepy. She looked up at the sky and watched the clouds blowing across it while Lauren settled down next to her. Chester came and curled up at her side. Lauren began patting him, her fingers accidentally brushing against Harper's arm. It made Harper shiver.

The thought of their friendship continuing when Lauren went home made her feel good, but she still wished things would never change. If she could spend every Saturday in this exact same way, she would be so happy.

CHAPTER TEN

They went to the lake the following weekend, and again the next. Lauren picked Harper up in the morning, and they drove out there to stay until sundown. Each time they spent the whole day talking, leaving their neglected newspapers and books spread out in front of them. The two of them took turns putting together picnic provisions, bringing leftovers or cooking for one another. Sometimes they would throw a Frisbee or ball for Chester to catch, and other times they would take him for long walks around the lake's edge.

During the second weekend, Lauren surprised Harper by following Chester right into the water. He had been chasing a ball close to the edge, then buoyed his strength and bounded in after it. Lauren didn't hesitate; she just waded right in to the dirty water like it was no big deal. When she walked out, she was soaked up to her waist. Harper had been laughing, but when Lauren came out with her shorts clinging to her skin Harper pretended to be engrossed in her book. Lauren sat on the bank in the sun to get dry and Chester sat beside her, shaking himself furiously.

After some time passed, Lauren came back to join Harper on the blanket. They lay on their backs, staring up at the sky. Harper was eating from a bag of chocolate-covered peanuts, and she held out the bag to Lauren, who took some and thanked her. They lay in companionable silence for a while.

"You know all about my family, but you've never told me about yours. I don't even know where you grew up. Do you see your parents much?" Harper asked. In her quiet way, Lauren was the sort of person who asked a lot of questions. Now that Harper thought about it, she realized it had been a very effective tactic at distracting her from asking much in return. When she did ask questions, Lauren usually found clever ways to deflect them and to turn the conversation toward other things.

Lauren looked down at her hands and rubbed at her palm with her thumb.

"You don't like talking about yourself too much, do you?" Harper asked.

Lauren shook her head.

"That's got to be hard. You must get asked a lot of questions in your line of work."

"I do. I've tried to keep my family life to myself but sometimes it feels like nobody cares about my privacy. I've forfeited my right to it, like if I wanted to get famous I should just suck it up."

"That's so unfair."

"I keep waiting for it to all come out. Like, some cousin is going to cash in and write a book or something."

"People are the worst. I respect why you'd want to keep stuff to yourself. I hope you know though, that I don't have an agenda here. I just want to get to know you better. If you want to tell me anything I'll listen, but whatever you say stays with me."

Lauren hugged her arms around herself. "I think I've known that for a while. Okay. I don't actually know where my parents are. They've never been around much."

"Did they raise you?"

"Sometimes. They were always splitting up and then getting back together, using me as a pawn when it suited them."

"Whom did you live with, then?"

"Whoever would have me—aunts, grandparents, friends. I'd just get settled, then one or the other of them would say they wanted me back. I'd have to go live in whatever dump they were staying at. They were really dysfunctional people, emotionally abusive, couldn't hold on to a cent. I had to grow up fast. It was all pretty bad."

"Do you mind if I tell you I really admire you for coming through all that?"

Harper put an arm under Lauren's neck, around her shoulder, and pulled her close. Soon she was lying with her head resting on Harper's chest, while Harper kept an arm about her. Lauren closed her eyes, resting an arm across Harper's waist.

"I know I'm a cliché, rags to riches and all that," Lauren said. "When it all comes out they'll make a great TV movie about me."

"I would never think of it that way. I think you're amazing," Harper replied. Lauren's self-consciousness was evident. Harper hoped she didn't regret opening up like this. Harper wanted to say so much more, but it would be wrong to put her feelings on Lauren right now, when she was so vulnerable. If Lauren missed having a close family, Harper wanted to offer to help fill that gap as much as she could. She could give Lauren whatever love she had missed out on, even if it were only as a friend.

"We're a sorry pair though, aren't we?" Harper asked.

"Everyone's got scars, I guess," Lauren said.

"Well, I like your scars."

Harper could only lie there for another minute or two before she had to move. She was becoming afraid that she was going to do something impulsive and stupid otherwise.

The next weekend at the lake, they had sandwiches, then Lauren reluctantly suggested they do some work. Since they had started hanging out more often, Harper had offered to help Lauren with her lines. Lauren was meticulous when it came to having them committed to memory, even though Sal was probably going to rewrite them. By now Harper was almost as familiar with the ever-changing script as Lauren was. At first, Harper had been self-conscious about saying lines from the script, but after a while she slipped into a variety of roles, including Lauren's character's mother and best friend. She didn't try to act, just read the lines and watched Lauren work. Sometimes she'd give Lauren tips on how to sound more authentically Southern. Harper liked to do it and Lauren had told her a million times how much it was helping her.

On the way out in the car, Lauren had been complaining about how she didn't feel challenged or excited by the scene that was coming up on Monday *at all*. She said it was an important scene for her character but that it bored her. When Harper asked for more information she had said that it was an important scene for her and Josh. It had been on the tip of Harper's tongue to ask whether the reluctance was about her past relationship with the leading man. Whenever the subject of Josh came up, Lauren always seemed indifferent. Harper wondered whether she truly didn't care or if she was just faking it because it was too painful.

Lauren pulled a face as she handed over the pages. "It's cheesy, I'm warning you."

"Are there any scenes in this movie that aren't cheesy?" Harper joked, looking over the script.

All it took was a glance for her to see that this was going to get weird for her. Words like "love" and "feelings" and "need" stood out on the page. Harper felt her face becoming hot. She had read Josh's lines before and found it funny to imitate his flat way of speaking, but she didn't think that would work so well this time. This conversation was more emotional, more overtly romantic than anything they had done before.

Harper didn't want to do it, but it would look strange if she refused to help now. She had to go ahead with it and try to not think about the words that were coming out of her mouth.

They began and Harper worked her way through it, line by stilted line. "If I stay here, you know what's going to happen between us."

"You shouldn't talk like that. Anyway, I don't think I understand what you mean," Lauren said.

"I think you do know. You've known it from the moment we met. You need me, like I need you."

"I'm afraid. Afraid of how I feel, afraid of what this all means. Don't you see that?"

Despite the awkwardness, Harper felt her usual awe at how good Lauren was. When Lauren spoke, the words seemed so much better than they were.

"Don't be scared of your feelings," Harper continued. "Let me in. Darling, I thought I knew what it was like to be happy before I met you. I thought striking oil was the biggest thrill a person could have. You're better than any oil. Just tell me how you feel, please." Harper could not keep herself from giggling at that line. "Better than oil? Seriously, you need to get Sal to change that. I've never heard anything so ridiculous."

Lauren nodded but then held a finger to her lips. Harper went back over the line, this time managing a straight face.

"I can't say it," Lauren said.

"You have nothing to be afraid of. I've never met anyone like you. You're safe with me."

"I think I'm falling in love with you," Lauren said, her eyes welling with tears.

Harper's heart lurched. For a second, she'd tricked herself into thinking that Lauren was actually speaking to her. Lauren usually held something back when they ran lines, but it didn't feel like that today.

"That's all I need. All I ever need," Harper finished.

They each fell silent and still. The words on the page rose up between them, the stage direction that they should kiss looming.

"It must be so strange making out with someone for a movie. I've always thought that would be really weird," Harper said, although in truth she had never given much thought to it either way.

Lauren kept her eyes on the page in front of her. "It's really not. People make a big deal of it, but it's so choreographed. Sex scenes are awkward because you have to take half your clothes off, but kissing's not that bad."

"Doesn't it depend on who you're kissing?" Harper asked. It must at least be strange for Lauren to have to kiss her ex-boyfriend in front of so many people.

Lauren shrugged. "Sure. I've had to kiss dudes with bad breath. That's annoying."

"I don't know. I'm not knocking that it's part of your job, but you're still actually kissing someone you don't necessarily want to."

"I promise it doesn't feel like that at all. It's mechanical. You do it a dozen times and it's so boring. Here, do the lines again and I'll show you."

"Okay, okay," Harper said, flustered.

She got to the pivotal moment, and again she paused. Harper held the script down at her side and looked at Lauren. Harper didn't know exactly what Lauren had meant when she said she would show her. Of course she wouldn't actually do it.

Lauren moved forward on the picnic blanket and cupped Harper's face in her hands. Harper was acutely aware of her own mouth, which was dry and nervous. She wet her lips with her tongue and saw how Lauren stared.

"Sometimes you'll put your hands like this so it hides your mouths a little from the camera," she said. "And they place the camera so you can't really see what's going on anyway."

"The magic of Hollywood huh?" Harper said shakily. She clutched her hands in fists at her sides, one of them still gripping the script.

"And you kiss with a closed mouth," Lauren continued.

"That's not true, I've seen people kiss with open mouths all of the time," Harper argued.

"Well yes, but it's very bad manners to use tongue. You just make it look like you are." Lauren smiled.

"And how do you do that?"

Lauren rolled her eyes and finally she leaned in. When her lips touched Harper's, Harper felt a charge through her whole body; she was sure that her lips had never felt so sensitive. She didn't know how much she was allowed to respond, and her confusion made her sit rigid and unsure. Lauren used her thumb to caress Harper's jaw. After a moment, she pulled back.

"Now open your mouth," she said in a whisper, and Harper felt breath on her lips. She obeyed.

Lauren's mouth was open against hers, and moving, and she understood what Lauren had meant. It felt as fake as Lauren had been describing, unsatisfying and strange. Yet there was so much underneath it. She could swear that she could feel Lauren holding back with the same force that she was. Harper's desire was intensifying by the second. She couldn't do this, she couldn't.

Soon she had taken Lauren's elbow with her free hand, to keep her close. Harper's tongue moved into Lauren's mouth. She heard Lauren moan softly once, when their tongues slid against one another's. The script in Harper's hand dropped with a rustle and she put a hand in Lauren's hair.

Harper couldn't believe how velvety and sweet Lauren's mouth tasted. She felt like she was never going to get enough of it, nor get enough of the way that Lauren was kissing her back. It was in a way that left no doubt that she'd wanted this just as much as Harper did. They fit together more perfectly than she had ever imagined they would.

They kissed for what felt like a very long time. Lauren eagerly kissed her, the two of them locked in a dance. There was no pretense anymore, no reason for them to act like this was anything other than what it was.

Harper's hands moved downward, rubbing along Lauren's arms. Her skin was so soft and smooth. Harper wanted to be on top of her. The need overcame her and she started to move Lauren backward, but stopped when she met unexpected resistance.

Lauren pulled back. When she looked at Harper desire was written on her face.

"What are you doing?" Lauren asked her, breathless.

"Nothing," she said, looking at an expression that scared her. She couldn't understand what had gone wrong. She didn't know what to say. "Did I move too fast?"

"No, I meant…don't worry about it." Lauren was pushing her hair out of her face self-consciously. "Chester, come here!"

Harper watched in confusion when Lauren began packing up the food containers. Because she didn't know what else to do she started to help, glancing at Lauren every few moments to try to work out what was going on.

"Are we going?" Harper asked.

"I think we should," Lauren said, her voice frightened.

"What's going on?" Harper asked. She was going over the kiss, trying to figure out if there had been any resistance or red flags before those last moments. There was nothing. Lauren had been kissing her eagerly one minute then freaking out the next. Lauren had been using the fake kiss as a pretext to really kiss her. That had been obvious. Even if Harper had been wrong about that, Lauren had still kissed her back for a good long while.

"I was just showing you, like I said," Lauren said.

"Lauren…" Harper said in disbelief.

"You got the wrong idea. I'm sorry. Let's just move on."

Lauren was folding up the blanket and refusing to look at her. It was disturbing how completely she was able to shut Harper out. It left Harper with no choice but to drop it. She picked up the picnic basket and walked over to Lauren's car with it, depositing it on the backseat. When she turned around, Lauren was nearby and holding Chester.

Lauren got into the car. The windows were still down. It had been hot on the way there, and they had both been putting their hands out into the breeze while Lauren drove. Lauren started the car and sat, waiting for her to get in. Harper knew she couldn't get into that passenger seat. The thought of being driven home by Lauren when things were like this was unbearable. She could only imagine the cold silence, and the awkward good-bye that waited for her at the end of it.

Harper walked around to the driver's side, not bending down. She didn't want to see Lauren's face again, not when Lauren couldn't even look at her. "I'll walk, thank you. I'll see you tomorrow."

Harper turned and walked away briskly. She could hear that the car wasn't moving but she walked on, not looking up when it finally passed her by.

CHAPTER ELEVEN

It was a long walk back to town and Harper didn't reach home until over an hour had passed. It was getting dark by the time she arrived. She was sweaty and tired, so she got into the shower. As she stood under the cold needles of water, she pressed her fingers to her lips. The sensation of Lauren's touch, of the gentle pressure of her mouth, hadn't left her for a second.

Harper tried to sort through the chaos. Tension had been building between the two of them for weeks. Though at times she had almost convinced herself that Lauren was just being friendly, her gut told her otherwise. She noticed the excuses Lauren made to touch her and be close to her, the looks they shared so many times, and the way Lauren's eyes lingered on her body. It was crazy to think that a heterosexual Hollywood starlet could be interested in her that way, yet Harper was positive that it wasn't all in her head.

Why had Lauren rejected her like that? And more importantly, why had she instigated the kiss if it wasn't something she wanted?

Harper hadn't wanted to see the truth but now it was right in front of her. Lauren had been messing with her, especially today. It was obvious that Lauren enjoyed Harper's company and her attention. It flattered her, and she encouraged it because it made her feel good about herself. The connection between them was real, no matter how you chose to define it. Still, the reality of that connection becoming physical freaked Lauren out. Harper had to accept the fact that she had been used for companionship, for distraction, and maybe even to help Lauren to get over her relationship with Josh. Maybe Lauren was just curious. It wouldn't be the first time a straight woman had acted interested in Harper after finding out that she was gay.

There was no chance things could go back to the way they had been. If Lauren tried to continue as if nothing had happened, Harper knew she wouldn't be able to deal with it. The attraction had only grown in the wake of that kiss. She was disappointed in Lauren, but she knew if given half a chance, she would go back for more. It had been too good between them to do otherwise.

Harper resolved that she should be aloof but courteous when she was dealing with Lauren. She wasn't going to allow things to become uncomfortable when they still had to work together.

The evening passed agonizingly slow. For the first time since starting, she hated the idea of going to work. It was all well and good for her to try to plan how she wanted to behave, but she couldn't control the way Lauren might treat her. Despite her plans, she knew that it would crush her if Lauren were cold toward her.

When Lauren didn't bring Chester to her office as usual, Harper wasn't surprised. Still, she had held a sliver of hope that she might look up any moment and see Lauren standing there. If only Lauren would come to her and apologize, and if only she could provide a reasonable explanation for why she had behaved that way. Harper wanted to believe that Lauren wasn't the sort of person who would mess with her deliberately.

Harper was thankful for the good fortune that they were out filming on location today. It meant that she could hide in her office until Sal called upon her to do something. Harper spent much of the morning staring blankly at her computer screen. She had felt too queasy all morning to eat.

It was occurring to her how much she was going to miss Lauren and the way they talked at work whenever they had the time. The absence left a hole that was going to make her days less fun, less exciting, less special.

The phone buzzed. Harper jumped. She knew it meant Sal wanted her to come to the set. They were shooting the romantic scene today. The whole thing was too surreal for words.

When she arrived, they were in the middle of a take, and she was forced to stand back and watch while Lauren and Josh mouthed the familiar, saccharine lines.

"I think I'm falling in love with you," Lauren said.

"That's all I need. All I ever need," Josh replied.

The handsome leading man and his co-star drew closer and kissed, plunging a knife into Harper's chest. Just yesterday, those lips had been kissing hers. Harper wanted to avert her eyes but couldn't. In all her life she had never thought of herself as the jealous type, but now she was seized with the childish urge to do something to interrupt filming. She had never felt much either way about Josh, but right now she had an intense dislike for him.

Sal yelled, "Cut," and the crew began setting up the next shot. Because Sal hadn't acknowledged her yet and she couldn't just interrupt, she was held captive to the scene all over again.

Lauren was in the middle of a sentence when her gaze darted over and caught on Harper. She flubbed her line. Their gazes held on to one another's while Lauren swore under her breath and apologized, but still she didn't break eye contact. Harper didn't know how to read her expression. Lauren was now as opaque as she had been when they first met, before Harper knew what to make of her. The intimacy had been stripped away. They were nothing but strangers once more.

At last Harper disengaged from the staring contest by turning to Sal, grabbing the chance to talk to him while the crew worked.

"Hey, Harper. We're about to break for lunch once we've tried a couple of takes of this shot. It's not working today." Sal lowered his voice for a moment. "There is no chemistry here and I need to figure out how to fix it. Can you go and get me a sandwich from the diner, please?"

"Of course." Sal's assessment was a surprise to her. Josh and Lauren looked like they were enjoying it well enough as far as she was concerned. She didn't look back at them when she walked away.

When she got to Joe's, Sue greeted her cheerfully when she walked in. "Sit down and have a cup of coffee with me!"

"I'd love to, sweetie, but I've got to get back. I'm just picking up lunch for the boss," Harper said.

"What's he having? I'll put the order in and you can at least sit with me while they make it up. You can see we're not busy," Sue said, gesturing around at the empty diner. It was too early for the lunchtime crowd.

Harper agreed and they sat down in a booth. It was a relief to be sitting across from Sue. It meant there were no loaded interactions or complications, no feelings other than innocent friendship. She had been neglecting her other friends far too much since she changed jobs. Harper hated to think about where that had gotten her.

They were chatting about Sue's husband when Sue looked over Harper's shoulder and her expression brightened. "Well, hello there, Ms. Langham."

Harper spun around in her chair. If the doorbell had chimed to announce Lauren's presence, she hadn't noticed it.

"Hello. Hello, Harper," Lauren said.

"Hi," Harper replied. Why had Lauren bothered to follow her? Sal had obviously asked for his sandwich loudly enough that Lauren had overheard where he'd asked her to go.

Sue leapt out of her chair. "I'm sorry, honey, I almost forgot I'm on duty! What can I get you?"

"Just a coffee and a salad to go, if you don't mind? I'm sorry to interrupt you guys."

Harper looked down at Lauren's hands. She was literally wringing them.

"Oh no, please," Sue said. "It's my job after all. I'll bring it over with your sandwich, Harper. And you make sure you stop by and see me again as soon as you can."

"I will, Sue. Thanks."

Lauren slid into the booth across from her. There was a long silence. "We need to talk. Maybe we could meet after work?" Lauren asked finally.

"If you need to say something, you can say it now," Harper replied. "There's nobody around to hear us."

Harper wished that Lauren would spare her whatever speech she was about to deliver, but they might as well get it over with. This morning she had hoped for an explanation, but she knew in her heart that all Lauren was going to do was to ask her to keep her mouth shut.

Lauren picked up a napkin and started fiddling with it. "I just wanted to apologize for my behavior yesterday. I was way out of line."

Harper hated that she wanted to reach across the table and take Lauren's hand. It scared her that she was ready to make a fool of herself all over again. Where Lauren was concerned, she had no willpower at all.

"Thank you," Harper replied, not sure what else to say. Was Lauren apologizing for the kiss or what had happened afterward?

"I would really like it if we could still be friends," Lauren continued. Harper thought the words sounded rehearsed. She'd noticed this before with Lauren, but now it struck her as disingenuous rather than cute. "It's very important to me. You've come to mean a lot."

Harper looked past Lauren toward the kitchen, at Sue and Jimmy clowning around while they worked. What she had with them was friendship instead of this aching longing, this shell of what could be. This conversation was about Lauren putting Harper in her place. Lauren was making sure that she knew they could never be anything more. It offended and insulted her, because there would never have been any need for it to be said if Lauren hadn't come on to her.

"Listen," Harper started. "Our friendship was important to me too. But I don't think it's a good idea for us to spend time with one another from now on."

"Was important?" Lauren repeated. She leaned forward, her hands inching toward Harper's. Then, just as suddenly, they retreated. "I really am so sorry. Please forgive me."

Harper sighed. Didn't Lauren understand that it would always hang between them? Lauren might say these words now, but she knew Lauren well enough to know that the situation couldn't be repaired so easily. Lauren would never really be comfortable with her again.

"Lauren, you're a wonderful person, but you're confused. I hope you figure out what it is that you want." Harper had spotted Sue coming toward them and she spoke more rapidly. "Don't worry. I'm not going to tell anyone about what happened. And let's not let this affect our working relationship, okay?"

"Okay," Lauren said with a crack in her voice. Harper felt the pricking of her conscience at how sad Lauren looked. She hadn't known that Lauren would take it so badly. Maybe she could have chosen her words more carefully, but there just wasn't time for that. Lauren suddenly pushed out of her seat and walked toward the door, jerking it open.

"Honey, you forgot your..." Sue started to tell her, but Lauren was already gone. Sue kept walking toward Harper with a curious look. "All that to not pay for a cup of coffee and a salad?"

"Oh, she asked me to take care of it," Harper lied. She paid Sue for both Sal's and Lauren's things and went to get back into her car. She sat for a moment with her hands on the steering wheel. Harper was one hundred percent sure that she'd done the right thing. It didn't change the fact that she felt terrible about it.

That afternoon and for the rest of the week, they avoided one another. It was only now that Lauren was staying away that

Harper grasped how often Lauren had pursued her company before. Lauren had often lingered in her office or found her in the halls to chat. Now Harper found herself scanning rooms to see if she were there, and looking at her doorway to find it empty.

A few days after their conversation at Joe's, Sal asked Harper to bring him a notepad from his office. When she reached him, she saw that he and Lauren were watching a laptop screen together, their heads drawn close. When Harper walked in, they both looked up at her at the same time. Lauren registered her presence and smiled at her, but it was hollow. After all the time they had spent together, Harper knew the difference between her real smile and this fake one. Harper couldn't bring herself to react to it at all, and she ignored Lauren in favor of talking to Sal. She could feel Lauren staring at her.

By the time the weekend rolled around, loneliness was gnawing at her. For a while she had looked forward to weekends so much, but now the days seemed empty and boring. It was a taste of what she would have experienced when Lauren returned to New York anyway. She supposed it was better that she become used to it now.

No matter how hard she tried to be pragmatic about the breakdown of their friendship Harper felt terrible. Visions of Lauren's smile, the real one, were so clear that it was like a photograph in her mind. She missed the way Lauren always laughed at her jokes as though they were the funniest things she had ever heard, on the easy way Lauren would lie back on the blanket with her hands under her head, as though there were nothing she would rather be doing than spending time with Harper at the lake.

She wondered if Lauren missed her even half as much as she missed Lauren.

CHAPTER TWELVE

Could a person sustain a broken heart from the ending of a friendship? It certainly felt like it to Lauren, because she had never hurt this much over the loss of a lover. After Harper had told her she didn't want to be friends, she just lay on the sofa and cried, while Chester crawled over her and tried to lick at her tears. She grabbed him and held him in her arms, knowing he was the one thing that could make her feel better. Harper didn't even think enough of her to hear her out. It was clear she had lost Harper's respect, and she was sure she would never be given the opportunity earn it back.

Lauren had been aware of how much she had screwed everything up but she'd hoped for a second chance. That day Lauren just wanted that kiss, and didn't care about the consequences. All the talk about kissing and the built-up tension made her lose her head. Initially, she lied to herself that if she kept up the façade of the kiss being about work it would be okay, but that pretense crumbled very quickly.

Kissing Harper was eye-opening. Throughout her acting career, Lauren had played at passion, aping the kind of feelings she had never experienced in her real life. She never even really believed that kind of hunger and magic was real. That all changed when the lust shot through her as she felt Harper's body pressed against her own. Lauren wanted to give in to it completely, but after a few minutes of blissful abandon she woke up to reality. Her actions made her feel so exposed that she would have done anything to put her guard back again, and for Harper to not see how much she wanted her.

In the morning at work her heart raced and her chest tightened with anxiety. Sal had picked up on the fact that something was wrong, but she couldn't imagine talking to him about it. She couldn't imagine talking to anyone about it.

Sal pulled her aside when she got back from the diner after chasing after Harper like an idiot. If she thought she felt bad before the lunch break, acting a love scene with Josh was going to be an even bigger challenge now. It had taken all of her nerve to go and talk to Harper. Harper's disinterest in working things out crushed her.

"Okay, I don't understand why you can't pull off this kissing scene. Normally I'd think it was Josh, but am I right in thinking it's you?" Sal asked.

"It's nothing. I'm just not feeling it, that's all. I'm tired," Lauren replied.

Sal put his finger under her chin. "I've always said that you create chemistry with anyone. It's one of your many great gifts as an actor."

Lauren tried to smile. "Stop flattering me, you know I won't fall for it."

"See, you're smart too. If you can't do whatever it is that you normally do, I'll tell you what I tell everyone else. I want you to visualize your ideal person. I just want it to be a person who you need to kiss more than you need to breathe."

Lauren noticed the way he used neutral pronouns, knowing that people might overhear. She would have been angry with him if he had referred to her sexuality in front of anyone, but it was a painful reminder that she could just never speak freely.

If only she needed to make that person up. For the rest of the afternoon, when she closed her eyes she thought of Harper's face coming close to hers, and of the sweet bursting of nerves in her stomach. It struck her as a sad and dysfunctional thing for her to be doing, but it also felt like the only way she could get through this. How she felt or how she got there didn't matter to anyone as long as she could turn in a good performance. Sal was happy with her by the end of the day. For now, that would have to do.

Over the next few evenings, Lauren lost count of how many times she picked up her phone to call Harper. If she could have just one more try, one more attempt at finding the right words. In the end, she screwed up the piece of paper with Harper's number that she kept near the phone, and then deleted it from her cell. It was the only way to ensure that she wouldn't break down and go against Harper's wishes. She kept having long imaginary conversations with Harper in her mind. Although Harper hadn't said a great deal that day at Joe's, she'd said enough for Lauren to know that Harper had her all wrong. The words kept coming back to her.

A few days after the events by the lake, she was walking toward Sal's office when Harper was coming out of it. Lauren's first instinct was to turn and walk away but that would make her look ridiculous. Lauren was frozen in place. She watched while Harper clocked her, her step faltering just enough for Lauren to notice it.

Lauren gathered her nerve and walked past her, looking over Harper's shoulder and not greeting her. An unexpected wave of anger had come over her because of how bad things had gotten between them. It made her want to ignore Harper, to make Harper feel as bad as she did. When Harper brushed past her, Lauren had an overwhelming impulse to reach out and touch her, to grab her by the waist and make her pay attention. When Harper passed, she turned around and looked after her, but Harper didn't look back at her.

After a long pause, she eventually entered Sal's office. "What did you want to see me about?"

"Hello," Sal said sarcastically.

"Hi. What did you want to see me about?"

Sal had his cell phone in his hand and he held it up. "Harper's just gone to the store to get me some potato chips. You want anything?"

Lauren scoffed. "Is that really necessary? Is she just here to play fetch for you all day long?"

Sal sat back in his chair and spread his arms wide. "Darling, are you going to pretend you don't have an assistant for the rest of time when you're not here? You're in a self-righteous mood today."

Lauren felt her face redden. She knew he was right. "Okay, sorry. Can we get to the point?"

"I don't think that scene I wrote with you and your best friend is working. I want you to go over it with me, get a female perspective."

Lauren looked up at the ceiling. "Sal, you ask for my opinion and then don't listen to it. I don't know why you bother. I'm just an actor, not the writer. You're the writer."

"You've written before, and a damn good script too. Besides, this way you'll complain less when it comes to the time we have to shoot it."

Lauren reluctantly pulled out her script and started running through the notes she had already made. As she had expected, Sal kept arguing back at her every time she suggested a change. She was so on edge already that she felt like throwing her script at him in frustration. "Why don't you ask Harper for her opinion again? You listen to her more than me."

"I will. She has a good head on her shoulders. I wish she lived in LA. Do you think she would move? She's one of the best assistants I've ever had."

"Uh-huh," Lauren said, feigning disinterest.

"Well do you think she would? Move?" Sal prompted.

"I don't know. Why don't you just ask her?"

"I'm asking you because you two are so tight. Jeez, what's gotten into you lately?" Sal asked.

"Nothing. And we're not that close, so I wouldn't have a clue."

"Oh, you're not screwing? I assumed you were," Sal said, like he didn't care one way or another.

Lauren tried to not react too much. At least she could tell him the truth. "No Sal, we're not."

Sal looked back at her. "I always see you two talking, and I heard you hang out on the weekends. Did you have a falling out? Is that why you're so grumpy?"

"No. I don't care about her enough to fall out with her. I was only hanging out with her because there's nothing to do in this town," Lauren said, beating back a rising panic. She didn't like that Sal had worked out what was going on. Maybe everyone knew.

"Me-yow," Sal said.

Not a moment later Harper reentered the room. Without a word, she walked over and handed the chips to Sal. There was no way that she hadn't heard when the door was wide open, and Lauren had been speaking at a normal volume. Lauren made eye contact with Sal, but he was either oblivious that Harper had heard them talking about her or didn't care. He never had been one to get concerned with people's feelings.

"Can I get you anything else?"

When Sal declined, Harper turned around and walked toward Lauren. Her eyes were steely. Lauren forced herself to withstand the glare, even though the right thing to do would be to act contrite. She wanted to follow Harper out of the room and explain that she had only said it to throw Sal off the scent, but she knew that Harper wouldn't understand.

When she was sure that Harper would be safely out of the way, Lauren excused herself from Sal's office, needing to be alone. The words kept running through her head and she couldn't stop thinking about how horrible she must have sounded.

The possibility of any type of relationship with Harper was slipping further and further out of her grip.

CHAPTER THIRTEEN

Things had gotten ugly between them, and Lauren hated it. It was uglier than either of them wanted, or would have previously been able to imagine. It was a jumble of hurt and resentments and sadness on either side, and it was a mess.

They were waging a secret war with one another, competing over who could ignore the other person in the most brutal ways. They were savage in their indifference toward one another. Nobody watching could ever notice it because it was too subtle to be perceived from the outside. When they did speak to one another because they had to, they would be coldly professional.

The effort of behaving in such a way wore on Lauren, and it never stopped hurting when Harper behaved in kind.

In the mornings, she walked past Harper's office. She could have walked another way, but she had become used to this route when she'd dropped Chester off every morning. The need to be near Harper despite their new awful dynamic wasn't a tendency that she wanted to examine too closely. Sometimes the door was open, and sometimes it wasn't. Sometimes Harper was at work already, and other times it was clear that the office was empty. It was hard for Lauren to know when she refused to look in lest their eyes meet. She saw shapes out of the corner of her eye and tried to work out what they meant.

Today the door was closed. She paused for a moment, trying to pick out the telltale sounds of keys tapping or music playing. It didn't make any difference, not really, but she liked to know whether Harper had arrived and was in her office. It gave her the illusion of control over her day to know if she were likely to run into her or not. Lauren was holding her coffee mug in one hand and gripping her handbag alongside a sheaf of papers in the other. There was a stack of paperwork from her manager that she hadn't been motivated enough to go through and she had decided that today should be the day she did.

Lauren's head was tilted toward the door. She couldn't hear a sound. She was just about to walk on when someone rushed past her in the hall. The light grip she had on her papers faltered and they started to slip from her hands. When she was trying to stop it, she forgot she was holding coffee. In her attempts to hold everything together, she lost it all. Lauren swore as coffee went everywhere, spilling all over her clothes. The door opened and there was Harper, standing over her. She swore again.

"What happened?" Harper said in her lilting voice, coming down to help her.

"I was walking past and someone knocked into me. Don't worry about it, I've got it," Lauren muttered. Her voice was unsteady, her eyes filling with tears.

"It's okay. Just let me help you."

Lauren finally looked up and had to avert her gaze quickly. Harper's voice sounded so kind just then. It sounded just like it had in the old days before hostility had sprung up between them. When she looked at Harper's eyes, she was lost in them again. Even when Harper didn't speak, you could read everything in her expression. In that moment, Harper was looking at Lauren like she cared.

When was she going to get over this? It seemed like putting thousands of miles between them might be the only cure. It made her feel helpless, and feeling helpless made her feel angry.

"No thank you, I don't need anything from you," Lauren answered.

Harper sighed.

"Yes?" Lauren said sharply.

"Nothing, I just...I'm trying to be nice to you and you're so rude all the time," Harper said.

"You are not nice to me. You ignore me every chance you get. And I'm just doing what you told me to and keeping my distance like you wanted. Make up your mind, I can't keep up with you," Lauren replied.

"I said I wanted to keep a good working relationship with you, not that I wanted us to ignore one another," Harper said in a harsh whisper. "And I heard that really shitty thing you said about me. I do have feelings you know. It's not all about you!"

"How the hell was I supposed to know what you wanted?" Lauren said, her voice rising. "You barely even let me speak to you!"

Harper reached toward her, touching her cheek so tenderly that Lauren's heart lurched. Harper looked around the hall and grabbed a handful of papers, then beckoned Lauren to come inside her office. When Lauren reluctantly did so, Harper closed the door behind them and retrieved a box of tissues from her desk.

Lauren placed the bundle of papers she had picked up onto Harper's desk and took the tissues, dabbing at the coffee on her skirt.

"Thank you," Lauren said. She could feel it rising up, that sense of tension between them that had been so thick and sweet sometimes. She had seen something in Harper's face when she had touched her.

"Look," said Harper. "I'm sorry if I upset you that day at Joe's, I just thought it was better for the both of us if we didn't continue the way we were. I was really not okay with what happened."

"Well, I'm sorry I put you in that position in the first place," Lauren replied. "But I don't know why you get to be the one who decides everything. You didn't give me a say, you just shut me down."

Harper held her hands out. For once, she was at a loss for words. "I'm telling you, I needed to protect myself. I wasn't trying to decide for you, I was just doing what I needed to do."

"Okay, but you didn't even hear me out. You've made all these assumptions about me. If you'd let me talk you might have felt differently about everything."

"I don't think I've made that many assumptions. I was just reacting to what you did."

This conversation was circular. Lauren wondered if Harper was ever going to understand. The fact that Harper was so calm only made her feel more irrational. All this talk felt useless and having Harper so close to her distracted her. She wanted Harper to comfort her again, to put her hands on her.

"It wasn't just that. The things you said…you really don't know anything about me. You think that you do but you don't," Lauren tried to explain.

"I don't think that's true," Harper said. "I thought we were getting to know one another pretty well. If I don't know you it's because you don't let me."

"That's not true. I let you in but you weren't listening. You thought I was dating *Josh*," Lauren spat out. She balled up a handful of tissues and threw them angrily in the trash.

"What does that have to do with anything? I mean, you never talked about him, why would I know the details?"

"See, that's what I'm talking about. You're like everybody else. You think you know something about me just because you read it on the Internet. I've never been with Josh."

Harper stared back at her. "I'm confused as to why believing you were in a relationship that the whole rest of the world thinks was real is a problem. I asked you about Josh and you didn't say a word about it. You were all secretive, I seem to remember. You had plenty of time to explain it to me if I was wrong about you two. We spent a lot of time together."

Lauren shook her head. "You're so smart but you don't see what's right in front of you."

Harper frowned. "Okay, can you just say what you mean? I have no idea what we're talking about."

Lauren took a deep breath. "I've never been with any guy. Think back over all the time we spent together, do you ever remember me once talking about an ex-boyfriend? Do you recall me ever expressing even a passing interest in a man? And even if I had, haven't you heard of bisexuality? I'm not bisexual for the record, but my point is that it doesn't seem to have occurred to you that I might have actually been genuine with you."

Lauren could barely hear herself speak over the pounding of her heart. She moistened her dry mouth and watched while Harper opened her own mouth in shock.

Harper knew at once that it was true, though she hadn't consciously allowed herself to think about it too much before. It was one of those things that you both knew and didn't know, that you deceived yourself into ignoring when contrary evidence was being presented to you all the time. When it crossed her mind that Lauren might like women in the same way that she did, she had dismissed it as wishful thinking.

Harper took a deep breath. "If you're gay, why didn't you just tell me that?"

"I never hid things from you. I told you things about my family that are a big deal for me. And all you take away from everything is that I'm *confused*."

"I didn't mean it like that," Harper hissed back at her. "It wasn't supposed to be some big insult. I was upset that you had messed with my head like you did."

In retrospect, Harper realized it was glaringly obvious. The way Lauren looked at her, smiled at her…kissed her. Of course Lauren was gay. She should have known.

But Harper was also mad, because she wasn't just "anyone." Harper knew what it was like to be scared to come out. She had grown up in small-town Texas for crying out loud. She thought she had proven that she could be trusted.

Lauren waved it all away. "I don't know why I'm even telling you this."

Harper was finding it hard to hold on to her anger, especially when she could hear the emotion in Lauren's voice. Seeing Lauren almost crying before they had come into the office had rattled her. This changed everything. It made her realize that she'd been so caught up in her own pain and wounded pride that she hadn't given much consideration to the idea that Lauren was hurting too. There was so much going on that she didn't know about.

Harper moved closer. "Don't say that. You can trust me. You've always been able to trust me, that's why I'm so mad at you for thinking you couldn't."

Harper cautiously put her arms around Lauren, watching for Lauren's reaction until she knew that she wasn't going to be pushed away.

It was such a relief to hold her. It was something she hadn't even realized she needed so much until she had it. Harper put her hand on the back of Lauren's head, feeling the softness of her hair. Lauren relaxed against her, arms moving around her waist. They stood together, silently. Harper pulled back and rested her forehead on Lauren's. Lauren's eyes were open, staring intently up.

At the same time, they each inched forward until their lips were touching.

This time there were no games, no pretending. Lauren gripped Harper's shoulders and kissed her slowly, as though she wanted to savor it. The floor was falling away from under Harper's feet. She leaned down into it, letting it take her over. When they broke apart they were both breathing hard. Lauren had put a hand on her collarbone. Harper could feel the touch of her fingers burning there.

"Can you lock the door?" Lauren said. Harper turned in a daze and did it.

When she turned back, she stood against the door and watched Lauren, who was gazing back at her. Up until ten minutes ago she had thought of Lauren as toxic, someone that she should avoid if she didn't want to have her head messed with. It scared her how quickly that perspective had shifted and she wondered if she should take some time to think about this. There was no question of stopping it, not now. She stepped forward. Lauren put her hand on the back of Harper's neck and pulled her close. Her tongue moved into Harper's mouth with a kind of sweet roughness.

The kiss quickly heated up, the two of them desperately trying to get closer to one another. Harper was shocked when Lauren pushed her backward against the desk, guiding her to sit on it. Lauren kissed her neck, lips and teeth grazing her gently.

"How could you not know I've wanted to do this as soon as we met?" The words were hot and close to Harper's ear. She closed her eyes. All of this time, Lauren had felt the same way. All of those looks, those touches, had been Lauren's way of telling her that she wanted her too.

Lauren's tongue slid slowly up her neck. Harper shivered before their mouths joined once more. Harper reached for Lauren's waist, holding her. Harper liked how Lauren, who always seemed so shy, was anything but shy right now. She knew exactly what she wanted and wasn't afraid to take it.

Harper knew what she wanted too but remained passive. Although Lauren was showing no signs of stopping, Harper was wary of being rejected again. The last time they had been together like this, she hadn't imagined it stopping either. Her fingers dug lightly into Lauren's sides in an effort to stop them from wandering.

They were so in sync in this moment that it was as though Lauren knew exactly what she was thinking. She took Harper's hands and pushed them upward, until Harper was cupping her breasts. Lauren stopped kissing her for a second, leaning up against her while Harper moved her hands over her. She could hear Lauren's quickened breath. Harper moved one of her hands and untucked Lauren's top from her skirt, pushing her hand underneath. The skin she found there was so smooth. Harper ran her hand around to Lauren's back, her fingertips caressing the soft flesh. Lauren had started kissing her again, her hips straining against her.

They came to an abrupt halt when there was a loud knock on the door and a voice called out. "Harper? You in there?" The doorknob rattled, twisting back and forth. Harper recognized Sal's voice. Lauren looked back at her in wide-eyed horror.

"Get behind the desk, I'll take care of it," Harper whispered. She quickly composed herself, grabbing a tissue to wipe Lauren's lipstick from her mouth. There was a second where she couldn't help but smile at the image of Lauren ducking guiltily behind her desk. She felt crazed, almost hysterical with the strangeness of what had just happened.

"Sal, I'm sorry. I forgot that I'd locked that. I spilled coffee all over myself and had to change," Harper said as she opened the door. She was surprised at how smoothly her voice came out.

"No probs. Can you type this up and email it to the address on this note?" he asked.

"Right away," she said, relieved when he didn't hang around at her door or try to come inside.

Lauren sheepishly rose from behind the table. "Well, that was a close call."

"It was." Harper raised her eyebrows at Lauren, who was tucking in her top and smoothing down her skirt. Lauren looked disheveled, her hair and clothes showing signs of what they'd been up to. Harper thought she'd never looked sexier, and wondered if it would be out of line to suggest that they pick up where they left off. The more logical part of her brain understood that the moment had passed. They were at work, aside from the fact that they had so much unresolved business.

They stood across from one another silently, a few feet separating them. Harper held up the pages in her hand at last. "I should probably get to this..."

"Oh yes, of course. People must be looking for me too. I should go," Lauren closed her mouth and opened it again. Harper willed her to say whatever it was that she wanted to.

Lauren's reticence was a sweet and integral part of her, but right now she wanted Lauren to keep being as bold as she had been a couple of minutes ago.

"Can you come by tonight?" Lauren asked. "Eight o'clock, if we're not shooting late?"

Harper nodded, knowing that the hours between then and now were going to feel like years. She buried herself in her work, and waited.

CHAPTER FOURTEEN

It was undeniable. For those many blessed minutes, Lauren's mind stopped working and she let the rest of her take over. The kiss was everything that she had been chasing for a long time and never managed to come close to finding. Intimacy had never been natural for her because she had never been able to trust and let go. Harper made her want to let go.

Now that she was alone, however, the certainty she had felt faded. Was it a bad idea to invite Harper over like that? Perhaps she was only making it more difficult for herself in the long run. Another fear elbowed its way into her head. All of that time when they weren't talking, Lauren had been afraid that Harper didn't care about her in the same way. Now that it had become apparent that Harper was at least attracted to her, she worried about what disappointments the future might hold. They had made no promises to one another. If something happened between them tonight, it would make it even harder when they had to part ways.

This couldn't really go anywhere. Harper would never follow her back to New York. The relationships Harper had with her father and brother were important to her in a way that Lauren had never experienced with her own family. It was obvious that Harper felt responsible for looking after everyone. Her sense of responsibility toward her loved ones was one of the things that Lauren admired most about her. And although Lauren had been enjoying staying in this town more than she could have ever imagined, there was no way she could stay permanently and still have a career. It was only a temporary bubble, a reprieve from the world.

She tried to quiet the chatter in her head and focus on the present. It was a lot like the first night Harper had come over, though she was even more nervous now. When she arrived home from work, she rushed to throw something together to eat and then showered quickly. Lauren couldn't help laughing at herself when it was time to get dressed, at the way she felt compelled to choose her underwear carefully. She was electric with desire from kissing Harper, her mind turning persistently to Harper's hands and mouth and what they could do.

When she opened the door, Lauren's breath stopped in her chest. Harper was wearing a white T-shirt and skinny jeans, her hair flowing loosely. Lauren felt like pushing her up against the nearest wall to kiss her. Instead, Lauren greeted Harper politely and invited her inside. When Harper came in, she stood with her hands in her pockets. There was a beat when Lauren thought Harper might kiss her or at least give her a hug, but she didn't move forward.

"Can we sit down somewhere and talk?" Harper asked.

"Sure," Lauren agreed with a sinking heart.

They sat down in the living room. Harper crossed her legs one way, and then the other, pushing hair behind her ears. Lauren started jogging her own leg up and down impatiently. She saw Harper looking at her leg, and then at her face. They both started laughing at the same time.

"Look at us," Harper said, shaking her head. "We're a mess."

Lauren shrugged, not wanting to give anything away until she knew where she stood. "I guess."

The silence rose up again before Harper broke it. "You make me really nervous."

It was impossible that Harper, a person who came across as so comfortable and at ease with herself, could be nervous because of her. Lauren shook her head. The tension was unbearable. Lauren was trying to imagine what would happen if she went over to her, if she knelt before her and threw herself at her feet.

"I'm going to go and get us both a glass of wine, give you time to figure out what you want to say to me. Does that sound okay?" Lauren suggested.

Lauren could feel Harper's gaze on her when she got up. They followed her as she stood, trailing up and down her body. Lauren felt it like a touch, her skin tingling.

Lauren stood at the kitchen counter and put her elbows on it, leaning her head on her hands to try to pull herself together. She knew that she had to deal with whatever Harper wanted to say, and her nerves were shot. She hoped she could keep herself from breaking down in front of Harper. Take it with dignity, she said to herself. You've endured much worse than this; you're going to be fine.

Lauren poured the wine, took a deep shuddering breath, and walked back into the living room. As she was putting the glasses down on the coffee table and stalling by fussing with the coasters to go underneath them, Harper stood up.

"You're not going?" Lauren asked. Was Harper just going to bail on her? After that day at the lake, she'd had the uncomfortable sense that it was easy for Harper to walk away from her.

Harper took Lauren's hand and pulled her forward until they were facing one another. "No."

Lauren's heart thudded like a drum as Harper's hand came to her throat and moved up to her cheek, the other drawing her in by the waist. Lauren's head fell back. She closed her eyes, sighing when Harper's warm mouth pressed to her lips. Lauren loved the way that Harper kissed her, fiercely and possessively, treating her like a precious thing. It made Lauren weak at the knees, because nobody else had ever made her feel so safe and so turned on at the same time. She didn't want Harper to ever stop touching her.

After a while, Harper pushed her toward the sofa. When she was sitting, Harper straddled her. She held Lauren's face in her hands and kissed her mouth and neck. Lauren could hear her own heavy breathing, no time anymore to worry, because she was too consumed by the feeling of Harper's body close to hers. Lauren ran her hands over Harper's back and pushed them into Harper's hair. How many times over the last six weeks had Lauren admired this hair, her skin, and the full lips that were kissing her?

Suddenly, Harper stopped. Lauren opened her eyes and stared up into Harper's face. Harper used a finger to trace a line around her lips, and over her chin.

"Are we doing the right thing?" Harper asked her.

Lauren looked at her solemnly. "I don't care."

"Come with me."

Walking to the bedroom with Harper gave Lauren a moment to take stock of the fact that she was aware of every nerve ending in her body. Her legs felt like they were made of liquid. For the first time since Harper had started kissing her, she had time to think about what they were doing. Old insecurities about her body were entering her mind, as were thoughts about how much more sexually experienced Harper might be than she was. She had been with a few women in her time, but she had never gotten to a place of open communication and true intimacy. How could you know if you were any good if you had never had that?

When they reached her room, Harper turned toward her. There was no mirrored doubt or hesitation written in Harper's gaze. Harper came toward her and grasped the bottom of her top, raising her eyebrows in a question. Harper lifted the garment over Lauren's head. Harper's eyes roamed over her body, her fingertips following them.

"You are so beautiful," Harper said. Lauren had heard that sentence many times from people who wanted something from her. It got thrown at her by people who said it all the time, about everybody. When Harper said the words, she believed them. Harper was the first person in a long time who actually saw her.

Lauren reached around to undo her own bra, watching Harper's eyes drop, the subtle change in her expression as she watched Lauren undress. Then Lauren reached forward and together they took off Harper's shirt and bra. Lauren touched her softly, her palms on Harper's breasts before gently pushing her forward to lie on the bed.

Lauren closed her eyes and reveled in the feeling of Harper's soft skin touching her own. They moved against one another, the friction of their bodies making Lauren moan. Part of her felt like she could be satisfied with just this, just kissing and never stopping, yet at the same time her whole being wanted what must come next.

Now and then Harper's hands would slide down her body, pulling her close by the hips or drawing sweet circles at her waist. Just when she needed it, Harper rolled her onto her back and trailed kisses down her neck and over her breasts. Lauren's back arched. Harper's fingers ran over her thighs under her skirt and came to rest lightly between her legs.

"What?" Lauren said breathlessly, impatiently, when her waiting yielded nothing.

Harper was looking down at her, her expression serious. "I feel like I almost want you too much."

In response, Lauren took Harper's hand and put it back where she wanted it. She heard the catching of Harper's breath. They quickly removed the rest of their clothes and Harper again positioned herself on top of Lauren, her hand moving down between them. Lauren's head was thrown back on the pillow.

Lauren opened her eyes. When she looked up, the way that Harper was looking down at her melted her. Her expression was awestruck, like Harper couldn't believe that they were here. Lauren couldn't believe it either. Lauren pulled her down to seek a kiss but rapidly lost focus when Harper's skilled fingers stroked her. Her hands grabbed at Harper's shoulders, her waist, her fingers digging into Harper's back. They looked into one another's eyes while they rocked against one another. When Lauren exploded into white light, she called Harper's name.

As soon as she had recovered, Lauren reversed their positions so that Harper was lying underneath her. Without hesitation, she moved downward, kissing Harper's stomach before she moved lower. Lauren was tentative for only a moment, because she could hear Harper's fast breath and she could feel Harper's hands on her shoulders. When she looked up and saw Harper's head thrown back and her mouth open in a moan, she let her apprehension go. She curled a hand around Harper's thigh. It was revelatory for her, the sensation of making someone who always seemed so in control break apart with pleasure.

For a while they lay together, staring up at the ceiling. No words felt adequate. Lauren had the curious sensation that she was changed in some way, that she wouldn't be able to look back after this. She would never be able to sleep with another woman without comparing it to this experience and to how she felt right now. Harper's fingers were lightly circling her arm.

When they made love again, it was slow and sweet. In the lost sense of urgency, they studied one another's bodies carefully until they were exhausted, and lay together. Harper was spooning her and she smiled into her pillow. They were quiet for a long time.

"How are you?" Lauren said, not knowing what else to say.

"How am I? I'm pretty good," Harper said dryly.

A smile stretched out over Lauren's face, and then she was immediately sobered by the thought that she had failed miserably at controlling herself. They had only papered over their issues, and maybe created more of them. Still she couldn't be anything other than ecstatic about what had just happened between them.

"What are we going to do now?" Lauren asked her.

CHAPTER FIFTEEN

Minutes and hours were slipping through Lauren's fingers like sand. They had wasted so much time.

All of their weeks of friendship had been special and they had led to this, so she couldn't regret them. What she did regret were those weeks during which they weren't even talking. They could have had more of this, even if they were yet to define what exactly "this" was. When she asked Harper what they were going to do, her words had been met with an anxiety-inducing silence. Lauren was conscious of Harper's fingers stroking her stomach, the flutter of her eyelashes against Lauren's bare shoulder. The physical closeness was comforting but she needed more.

At last, Harper had answered in an optimistic tone. "Let's enjoy the time we have together. Can't we just do that?"

Lauren had wanted to hear a declaration of how Harper felt about her. She had also hoped to extract a promise from Harper that they would find a way to make this work out. Harper's answer was disappointing but she clung to the fact that they would at least have this time together, that Harper's words implied there might be more nights like the one they had just shared. Lauren had never been the type of person who could throw off worries about the future, but for the sake of enjoying this, she would have to try.

"Okay," she had replied, covering Harper's hand with her own.

That night Lauren couldn't remember when she finally drifted off to sleep, though she knew that they woke up together in the early hours. They reached for one another and made love once again before each drifting off again. No word was spoken—only the sounds of moans and breathing. The quiet intensity of it was something Lauren had never known before.

It felt like she had only been asleep for minutes when Harper woke her again to say that she'd better get going. She had promised her little brother she would take him to get some new clothes for school. Lauren sat up sleepily, pulling the sheet over her naked body, while Harper sat on the edge of the bed.

"Go back to sleep," Harper said.

"Okay," Lauren agreed, as though she could even stay awake if she tried. Harper laughed at her and then leaned in to kiss her one more time. At least that had been the plan, but Harper pulled the sheet away and kissed her everywhere until Lauren gasped in pleasure with the sheet balled in her fists.

When Lauren woke up again, the afternoon sun was beaming through the windows. Those moments in the morning had a dream-like quality to them when she looked back; in fact, the whole night did. But there was no denying it was real. Lauren stretched and felt the delicious tiredness in her limbs. If Harper was beside her right now, her fatigue would drop away and she would be ready again.

They had not made any solid plans to see one another. Things between them had changed so rapidly that it left her uncertain about what the protocol might be. Because she didn't know what to do, she took no action at all. When she finally rose from bed, she cleaned the house and cooked herself an early dinner. She was ravenous. As she ate, she dreamily went over what she had done the night before, and what had been done to her.

By the time it reached ten o'clock, she still hadn't done anything much except for sitting and staring at the television. Lauren flicked mindlessly through the channels, but nothing could hold her interest. She was pulled toward Harper like a magnet. Chester was snuggling up to her on the sofa and she decided to take him out, because she had missed their morning walk. She clipped on his lead and let him outside, knowing where she was really going. They walked straight to Harper's house, Chester happily trotting along beside her. When they arrived, she pulled her phone out of her pocket.

"Hey," Harper's warm voice greeted her. There was something in it that she hadn't heard before, a playfulness that acknowledged the change in their relationship. Relief washed through Lauren when she heard how welcome her call was.

"What are you up to?" Lauren asked.

"Oh, nothing. I'm kind of bored actually," Harper replied. "What about you?"

"Nothing either, really. I'm just out walking Chester."

"Really? It's late. Where are you?"

"Actually I'm across from your house," Lauren said in a rush. When the phone in her hand went silent, she winced and squeezed her eyes shut. She put her fingers to her forehead. "I'm sorry, is this completely weird? I didn't mean to seem like a stalker or something, I just thought if you weren't busy…"

"Lauren," Harper cut her off, laughing at her in that way she had that didn't seem mean. "I'm just quiet because I'm putting on my shoes. I'll be out in a minute."

They fell into bed as soon as they got back to Lauren's place. Lauren could have wept with the thrill of it, from Harper's hands on her in the dark, from the wordless ecstasy, the feeling of coming home again.

Afterward, Lauren rolled onto her side, pulling Harper's arm with her. Lauren smiled to herself. It had never felt so good to be in someone's arms. Gentle fingers played with her hair.

"So, what's the story with the Josh stuff?"

"Ugh, do we have to talk about Josh now?" Lauren said. She started laughing at Harper's bad timing. Harper's voice had been so sweet and low in her ear, but there was nothing sexy in talking about Josh. "Have you just been dying to ask me that?"

"Sorry, but yes I have," Harper confirmed. "Spill."

"There's nothing to tell. There were rumors for no good reason, because we were hanging out while shooting. My team loved it because nobody wants me being outed, so we agreed to let it happen. Josh doesn't really care because he's got no plans to settle down with anyone any time soon. You'd be surprised how often this sort of stuff happens."

"It must be hard for you though. Having to hide who you are," Harper said, giving her shoulder a squeeze. "I wish I'd picked up on it myself and made it easier for you."

"That's okay."

"I can't believe how blind I was."

"It's not your fault that I didn't tell you. I just hope you know I'm not ashamed of who I am or anything like that. I mean, I only hide it because I feel like I have to. Once you get used to something like that, it's hard to break out of it."

Harper sighed against her ear. She rolled Lauren onto her back and looked down at her. "I'm really sorry I've made you feel like you have to justify yourself. I should never have said those things that day at the diner."

"It's okay. I'm just telling you, that's not me. I've always been clear about what I want. This is just a really strange business."

"I don't judge you at all. I can't imagine what it must be like to have all those eyes on you. I was hurt when I said that."

"I'm sorry," Lauren said, remembering the dejected way Harper had helped her pack up after the picnic.

"It's okay. I'm definitely not hurting now," Harper pointed out. Lauren put a hand behind her neck and pulled her down for a kiss.

They replaced their old routines with new, more secretive customs. Most nights Harper pretended to go to bed, saying good night to her indifferent brother and father, before crawling out of her window. It made her feel like a teenager, only she never had this much fun when she actually was in her teens. Sometimes she would walk to the cottage and Lauren would be waiting for her. Other nights Lauren would sit in her car with the engine idling at the end of the street, and they would go out driving. Harper loved those nights the best. There was the balmy night air, her hand trailing out the window, tracing shapes in the wind or on Lauren's thigh. There was the way that Lauren would shoot longing looks at her, and take her hand while she was driving. Harper felt drunk with happiness.

Once they traveled so far that Harper suggested they pull over at a motel next to the highway rather than drive all the way back to the cottage. Lauren hid in the car while Harper checked in, so that the motel clerk wouldn't recognize Lauren. They busted into the room giggling. Harper had pretended her husband was waiting for her in the car.

"Oh, I sure hope my husband doesn't find out I'm with you in this flea-ridden motel," Harper joked. "If only we had a nice cottage we could go to in order to conduct this affair!"

Lauren pushed Harper down onto the hard and creaky bed. "We don't need a nice mattress, not when I'm going to do such nasty things to you on it." She bit Harper's neck, laughing.

No matter what they did, the evenings always ended in that same way, with them in one another's arms. When they weren't in the cottage, they made love in the car, parked in darkened places on the side of the road, on the picnic blanket at the lake, and even at work in an empty room. Harper didn't think she had ever felt such easy affection with anyone. She was comfortable with suggesting anything, at any time. Lauren's desire and willingness always matched her own.

It wasn't just the sex that made their time together so good. Harper loved the intimacy of their conversations; the way they'd lie together and talk all night about their lives. She wanted to learn everything she could about Lauren, wished to study her like a book, fascinated by how her mind worked.

"So how is that you've never been in love? You've just never met the right girl?" Harper asked her one morning. It hadn't escaped her notice that Lauren often changed the subject when it came to relationships. She had never mentioned ex-girlfriends or old lovers at all.

"Why, do you think it's strange? I'm not *that* old," Lauren said.

"No, of course I don't think it's strange. You must have broken a few hearts though. You're so very dreamy," Harper said. Lauren lifted her head and smiled at her.

"Is that how you think of me? Like a heartbreaker? I don't think so."

"You're so modest. Another thing that makes you lovable." Lauren gazed back at her, those clear penetrating eyes looking at her as though waiting for something. Regardless of how well she was beginning to know Lauren and how much Lauren had been opening up to her over the last weeks, there were still times when Harper found her eyes utterly unreadable.

Lauren broke away and lay back down. Harper wasn't sure whether to be worried that she might have hurt Lauren's feelings, or at least made her self-conscious.

"I'm glad you haven't, anyway," Harper said, to try to smooth it over. "Because then you might not have given me a chance. You might have some high-powered Hollywood executive wife or something."

Harper smiled when Lauren cuddled into her, throwing a leg over her waist and kissing her neck. "You're right. You're incredibly fortunate," Lauren said drolly.

"I am," Harper agreed.

Harper spent each day at work walking on air. Things went more smoothly than usual. She was so happy that there was no problem that she couldn't solve. She loved the quiet moments she found with Lauren, the deliciousness of running into her unexpectedly as they went about their days. All it took was a look for her to understand how much Lauren wanted her at any given moment. They didn't need to talk to communicate about that.

"You're in a good mood," Sal observed one day in her office.

"Just digging working for you, that's all," Harper said. She did love working for him. He didn't need to know the reason.

"About that. I've been wanting to ask you if you would consider staying on. I'd be happy to pay for your relocation costs to LA, help you get set up."

The question brought Harper out of her reverie. It was a great offer, but it could never work. It would take her even further away from her plans, the half-formed ideas she had about returning to New York one day. If she took on a more permanent role as his assistant, maybe she would never get back there. Besides, there was no way she was ready to leave her family.

"I'm sorry Sal, I just couldn't move right now. The offer means the world to me, though. Thank you."

Sal shrugged. "That's a shame. Whatever makes you happy though, kid."

Harper looked away from him. There was only thing that was making her happy, and she could never really have it.

CHAPTER SIXTEEN

When the time came that they only had one week left to be with one another, Lauren was a basket case. She felt jumpy and restless, especially when she was away from Harper. It would help if she knew that she could stay in town even for a little while after the shoot finished, but there was no way that her schedule would allow for it. There would barely be time for a day off in New York before she would have to get to work promoting *Empty Nests*, a family drama she had shot the year before. Doing press had never been one of her favorite parts of the job, and she felt like doing it now less than ever.

She wanted to ask Harper again if their relationship was going to lead anywhere, but she kept biting back the words. Harper had answered her once already, and Lauren was scared that her reply might not have changed. Harper was a forthright person; if she wanted something from Lauren, then Lauren was sure that she would ask. So Lauren had been doing her best to act like the situation was no big deal for her. When Harper complimented her, she didn't know how to take it. She could never tell if Harper was just physically attracted to her or if her feelings ran as deep as Lauren's own. Recently Harper had talked about how lovable she was. Lauren didn't want to hear that she was lovable. She wanted to know that she was loved, that Harper loved her.

It was difficult to talk about never having loved anyone when her feelings for Harper had rendered that a lie.

Now it was Friday night. She wanted to shake off her worries, because knowing they had the whole weekend together made her determined to cherish every free moment they had.

Lauren had barbecued some burgers, and they ate them on the back porch, watching the setting sun.

"You know, you're the best cook I've ever met," Harper said, licking sauce from her fingers.

"It's just a burger," Lauren said. She reached over and wiped a smudge of sauce from the corner of Harper's mouth.

"Yeah, but it's an amazing burger. It's the way you do it. You have magic hands."

Lauren held up a hand and wiggled her fingers around, raising her eyebrows suggestively until Harper laughed. It was so hot that Lauren could feel the back of her shirt sticking to her skin with sweat, droplets of it running down her legs. She had brought out a pitcher of iced tea that they polished off quickly. Harper pulled a chunk of ice from her glass and ran it over Lauren's collarbone. Lauren shivered at the cold and grabbed her hand, pulling her close.

The two of them sat until after dark looking out on the backyard, kissing. Lauren loved the way Harper put a hand on her chest, sliding it up her neck.

"Want to go in to bed?" Lauren asked.

"Not just yet. Why don't we go to the lake?"

"Right now?"

"It'll be gorgeous out there right now."

They drove out and parked, the moon so bright that they didn't need to leave the headlights on. The black water pooled out in front of them. Harper ran over to the bank and quickly pulled off her shoes, sinking her feet into the cool depths below.

She sighed with pleasure. Lauren joined her. Harper put her hand down at the same time as Lauren did and they linked their fingers together.

"This was a very good idea," Lauren said.

"I'm full of good ideas," Harper agreed.

Harper put her head down on Lauren's shoulder, nestling in, and Lauren put her arm around her. Lately a feeling of impossible tenderness had stolen over her every time Harper did something like that. It made her feel like Harper wanted to be *hers*, like they belonged to one another and both knew it.

For a second she truly let the emotions in. She had never felt this way before, not even close. For the past few weeks, she had been falling harder and harder. She had been sure for a while now that she was in love. It still struck her as miraculous that she could kiss Harper whenever she wanted. And yet there was a huge part of her that was always waiting for it to be taken away from her.

"Can I ask you something?" Lauren blurted. Harper nodded against her shoulder. "What did you think of me when we met?"

"It might be best if I don't answer that question," Harper said.

"Why not?"

"You just seemed a little aloof the first few times we met."

"Oh. Is that all? Well, that's because I was trying to not show that I was into you." Looking back on those days made her nostalgic. Though she hadn't known it at the time, it had all been building toward this moment: Harper's head on her shoulder, Harper's arm around her waist.

"I thought you meant when we first met. At the diner, when I served you. Do you remember that?" Harper asked.

"That is what I meant."

"Did you think of me like that right from the start?"

"Yes. I was like a deer in the headlights, I know. I couldn't get over the way you looked. How beautiful you are."

"Oh, come now. You're just sweet talking me."

Lauren wished she were. If only she didn't feel this way, it would all be so much easier. She wouldn't feel so heartsick at the thought of leaving Harper behind.

"You're serious aren't you?" Harper said. "You were being coy with me. I wish I'd known that back then."

"When did you start to think of me in that way?" Lauren persisted, fishing. She wanted to hear something real from Harper, anything that she could hold on to when she was lonely and they weren't together anymore.

Harper reflected for a moment. "That day in the park, when you came and started talking to me. I'd always thought you were beautiful, but that was when I started to get a crush on you. That was when I realized how sweet you are."

Lauren was grateful Harper couldn't see her face. There was nothing negative about what Harper was saying, yet it played into her worst fears. She didn't like thinking that what Harper felt for her was just an infatuation. It was difficult to hear that Harper hadn't experienced the same heart-slamming revelation that she had. If this were just a dalliance for Harper, Lauren knew it would ruin her. Lauren could see any hope of a future for them receding even farther into to the distance.

Lauren sat up straight and pulled her feet out, her mood turning suddenly as black as the water in front of them.

"You okay?" Harper asked.

"Yep. Just want to get back," Lauren said, trying to not sound as flat as she felt. She stood up and brushed off the seat of her shorts, holding out a hand to help Harper up.

Harper stood up and Lauren could see her questioning eyes in the moonlight. They stood facing one another. Harper tucked Lauren's hair behind her ear.

"Don't hold it against me that I didn't see you for what you are right away," Harper said. "You always were a bit mysterious. I've liked getting to know you; it's been the best thing about all this. Feeling like you're letting me in."

Lauren was struck again by the feeling that Harper understood her more than anyone else ever had. It was like she could read the turn of her every mood, could gather the meaning of every silence. There was no chance of hiding things from her. It could be scary, but she was relieved that she didn't always have to say things in words.

"I don't hold it against you," Lauren said and shrugged.

Harper held Lauren's face in her hands and placed one sweet kiss on her lips. "Okay. Just don't think that it means that I don't love you. I love you."

Lauren couldn't answer right away. Everything she was feeling must have been etched plainly on her face, but she was so taken aback that she let the chance to reciprocate melt away. Harper grabbed her hand to pull her toward the car.

It wasn't until later that night that she replied. They were in the moments between sleep and waking, their naked bodies in a loose embrace.

She had never said the words before to anybody. Still it wasn't surprising how easily saying them came to her now. After all, she'd wanted to say them for a while.

"I love you too."

CHAPTER SEVENTEEN

A wave of melancholy stole over Lauren when she woke up. She put her arm out, and then her leg to confirm her suspicion that the bed beside her was empty. Given how short a time they had known one another, it was strange to think that Harper was the person who had most consistently shared her bed over the past few years. As she shook off the fogginess of sleep, she realized that Harper hadn't left—she was just in the kitchen. Lauren could hear the rattling of pots and pans. It made her feel better, but only a little bit.

There was that ticking clock again. Their last weekend together.

When Harper came in bearing a mug of coffee, Lauren smiled weakly at her. The smile became real and widened when she took in Harper's outfit. Harper was wearing a tank top and her underwear, but she had tied an apron over them. It was a very old-fashioned one that had been hanging from a hook by the stove, lending the house one of the rustic touches that she loved so much.

Harper leaned over her and kissed her good morning. Lauren wrapped her arms around Harper, the pleasure of it taking her over as it always did.

"I've got to get back to the kitchen. I'm making you a big Southern breakfast, biscuits included."

"That sounds amazing. Can I help?"

"You're a damn Yankee, so no thank you, ma'am," Harper said, exaggerating her accent. "You can stay in here and drink that coffee and relax."

"If you say so," Lauren agreed. She watched appreciatively when Harper turned to walk away, revealing her bare thighs.

Lauren stretched and looked up at the ceiling, frowning. She was ruining what precious time they had left with her bad mood, but she couldn't help being this way. Again she resolved to shake it off, to be in the moment and enjoy herself. Harper was good at picking up on her mood and she would definitely ask what was up if Lauren kept feeling grumpy. It didn't sit well with her, the idea of Harper remembering her as clingy or negative. She wanted to be fun-loving and carefree in the same way that Harper was.

Lauren recalled the moment that Harper had told her that she loved her the night before. Thinking about it gave her an overwhelming jumble of emotions, none of them terribly clear or distinct.

Lauren reached for the coffee Harper had left on the nightstand. Her hand passed over Harper's phone.

As soon as she looked at it, she knew what she was going to do. Harper had always been clear that she understood the deal, that what was happening between them needed to be a closely guarded secret. Harper had been discreet at work, and Lauren had never needed to explain how they had to act any time they were in public. Harper was a perceptive person who picked up on everything without needing to be walked through it. Still, Lauren couldn't shake off the worry that Harper might have told a friend or a family member something that might make them wonder.

Lauren listened for the sounds of Harper working in the kitchen and was reassured that she wouldn't be disturbed. Now that she had allowed herself to think about it at all, her paranoia started to feel like an unspooling thread. Had Harper ever done anything stupid and reckless, not fully understanding the risks? Was there even the slightest possibility that Harper would ever use what she knew against Lauren? Everything in her didn't want to believe it, but people were unpredictable. Harper was in a strange position in her life. It had never occurred to Lauren for a moment to look down on Harper, but she was a lawyer working what must feel like a menial job. Did Harper ever dream of something more, things that Lauren's money could give her? She wished thoughts so ugly and toxic had never crossed her mind, but once they had, they weren't going to go away. Lauren grabbed Harper's phone.

Lauren scrolled through the text history quickly, seeing mostly her own cryptic messages. They only used text messages to arrange meeting times and places. There were messages between Harper and other people too. Though she couldn't see anything that concerned her at first, she started going through the messages more carefully. By now she wasn't even sure what she was looking for, because it had occurred to her to wonder if there were other women. Even the thought of Harper having a flirtation with another woman bothered her more than she would have thought imaginable.

"What are you doing?"

Lauren jumped at the sound of Harper's voice. She had become so absorbed in her task that she hadn't noticed it when the noise from the kitchen disappeared. Now that her focus had shifted back, she could feel Harper's eyes on her. When she met them and saw Harper's expression, everything felt like it was plunging downward.

"Oh. Nothing. I was just looking at the time." Lauren cringed at her own lie.

Harper's eyes deliberately cut across to the clock on the nightstand. She moved closer and sat on the bed while Lauren exited the message list to cover up what she had been looking at. She forced herself to do it casually, trying to not look as panicked as she felt. When she was putting the phone back she kept her eyes averted, full of shame.

"Why are you going through my phone?" Harper's tone wasn't accusatory or angry. Anything would be easier for Lauren to deal with than Harper's profound disappointment in her. Lauren hadn't been under any illusion that Harper would buy her lie, but she had hoped that she would at least *pretend* to believe it so they could drop the matter.

When Lauren didn't answer, Harper continued. "What did you think you were going to find exactly?"

"Nothing. I don't know," Lauren replied, shaking her head.

"Are you worried that I'm seeing someone else? Is that it?"

"No."

"Then what is it?"

Harper could be stubborn, and Lauren had a feeling that if she didn't say something true Harper was just going to keep asking her until she did.

Lauren leaned toward Harper, but she was too afraid to reach out and touch her. "I'm sorry. I just had this silly thought that there might be something in your phone linking you to me. I know you'd never deliberately do anything. I get paranoid sometimes."

Harper stared straight ahead. "So you couldn't just check with me or talk to me about it?"

"I know it was a weird thing to do. But haven't you ever done that? Gone through someone's phone or looked at their diary or whatever?"

"No. I haven't ever done anything like that. What you're saying is that your privacy is more important than mine. That's what it sounds like to me."

Lauren was at a loss for words. Harper was really angry, more than she would have expected. To think that she had just been worrying about not being cheerful enough in their last days together. That should have been the last of her worries. It was nothing in comparison to this.

"It's not like that at all. I don't think I'm more important than you. Can we just forget about it? Chalk it up to my being a neurotic actress type?" Lauren said, trying for lightness.

"You don't trust me," Harper said. "You never have, have you?"

"Of course I do!" Lauren replied. It was beyond her to explain it right now, but there had always been a tug of war between blind belief and suspicion. Maybe she wasn't capable of the type of love in which she wouldn't have a skeptical thought. Skepticism was her default mode, especially after recent events, and even before that, too many people had wanted things from her for too long. Yet her natural mistrust of other people didn't diminish her feelings one little bit. She thought the world of Harper. In fact, she thought too much of her, and that had always been the problem.

"You never wanted to tell me you were gay in the first place and now you're going through my phone looking for what? Messages to a tabloid journalist? References to a secret sex tape?" Harper scoffed.

"It's not that stupid. It's happened to me before," Lauren replied. When Harper stared at her in confusion, she knew she had to explain herself. If Harper knew more about her history, then maybe she would understand and they could put this behind them.

"I was blackmailed, by a woman. It's not a nice story. I guess it's scarred me in a way, makes me think stupid things. You don't know what it's like to be in my position."

Harper's face was blank. Lauren picked up the pillow and softly punched her fist into it, unsure of what to do with her hands. She had hoped that she wouldn't ever have to tell anyone about those pictures ever again. In her mind's eye she could see them and it made her feel panicked, as though the images could reappear in front of her at any instant.

"I don't know what it's like to be in your position, that's true. You could try just telling me."

"Okay. I was dating this woman I met at the gym. Angela. She was an actor, wanted me to mentor her or whatever. I thought she was okay because we had mutual friends so we went on a couple of dates. I wasn't that interested in her but she was kind of pushy. She wanted me to hook her up with powerful people, agents and stuff. That sort of thing happens all the time."

"And you slept with her?"

"Yes. That's what I'm trying to tell you. It only happened once and it wasn't good, didn't feel right. I thought she must have felt the same way. I never thought she really cared about me as a person, so I didn't think the whole thing was a big deal. But when I tried to break it off with her…"

"That's when she blackmailed you?"

"Yes. She had pictures that she'd taken of me when I was asleep. She was in them too. It was obvious what was going on. So, I had to pay her to make it all go away. I had to ask my manager for help because she came back asking for more money. It was the most embarrassing thing I've ever gone through. I still don't understand why anyone would do that to another person. That's why I need to be so careful. It made me feel like anyone could do that to me, like there's nobody safe."

"Including me."

"Not exactly, it's not really like that. I promised myself before I came here that I was going to take a break from seeing anyone for a while, and get my head together. But I couldn't stick to it, not after I met you."

"I'm sorry all of that happened to you, but that has nothing to do with me," Harper said. "How could you think that of me?"

Lauren realized that Harper was on the verge of tears. The awareness that she was making Harper so upset made her disgust over the photos feel trivial. Lauren hadn't known that she was capable of hurting Harper that much.

Lauren put her hand on Harper's shoulder, then moved it to Harper's back and rubbed gently. Now she wondered why she had even tried to defend herself, instead of being more focused on how Harper was feeling. When Harper looked at her, she understood that she really had made a grave error. The color had drained from Harper's face.

"You were always so reluctant to get involved with me. I can see now why. Do you really think I want your money? Is that why you're so suspicious, because of what I do? By your standards, we're really poor."

Harper moved away from her. It was just half a foot or so, but it was enough for it to hurt badly.

When Harper said the words, they sounded so wrong and so far-fetched that Lauren felt a fresh wave of horror at her own actions. Lauren was sitting quietly and trying to think of a way to set this all right, when Harper got up from the bed. Lauren said Harper's name and moved to follow her.

"I had all these ideas about this weekend," Harper said, her back turned, shoulders hunched.

"Me too. Please, I want to spend this weekend with you. Let's still do whatever it is that you want. I'm up for anything," Lauren pleaded.

"I had hoped you could meet my dad and brother tonight for dinner," Harper said.

"I'd love to. It would mean a lot to me to meet them. Please, forgive me and let's just have this weekend."

"Well, I don't think that it's a good idea now. I don't think so at all."

"Don't say that and then not let me do it. Why tell me at all?"

"Sorry," Harper said, then paused. "Why am I apologizing to you?"

"Because now you're just being cruel," Lauren said. She had always wanted to meet them but had never pushed the issue, knowing there must be reasons why Harper hadn't invited her over. Harper was pulling things out of the small bag she had brought over with her and took out a pair of jeans and a shirt. Lauren noted the way that Harper kept her back turned while she finished dressing.

"I'm not being cruel on purpose. It's just, what's the point anyway?"

The question and the way it was posed were devastating. It cut right through her. Lauren knew her behavior was beyond wrong, but what they had together should transcend their situation. Their different backgrounds didn't matter, nor did the fact that they lived miles apart. Lauren would care for Harper always, regardless of whether they even saw one another again. The point was that this had meant everything to her and if Harper felt the same, she wouldn't leave.

It was impossible to watch Harper go. Lauren only followed her halfway to the door before she turned back. She went back to the bedroom and laid down, her head and heart full of everything that had just happened. She tried to go back to sleep but couldn't. She tried to not think about the fact that her future felt pretty bleak right now. She couldn't do that either. It was pathetic that she was hanging so much of herself on another person, but it could not be otherwise, not after everything that had happened. At the very least she would have hoped for a good ending for the two of them, something that might give her hope that they would meet again.

When she got up hours later, she was tearful at seeing the breakfast Harper had made. It looked cold and sad, all laid out with not a bite taken out of it. Things should have been so different today. She cleaned it up, saving what she could and eating a bite here and there, but throwing most of it in the trash.

Lauren sat on the sofa. Chester, sensing her distress, curled up on her lap and raised his head to lick her face. Lauren patted him, feeling guilty that she hadn't taken him out today.

It was difficult to have to take such a good look at herself and not like what she saw. Her insecurities were toxic. She had finally met someone special, someone who even wanted to be with her, and she had screwed it all up with her doubts. When was she going to stop sabotaging herself and just let things work out for once? It made her sick of herself, but it also made her want to fight.

Harper wanted her to meet her family. No girl had ever wanted that from her. There was nothing Lauren would rather do.

At last, she picked up her phone and typed out a message. At this point, she couldn't make things any worse.

CHAPTER EIGHTEEN

When Harper opened the door and saw Lauren standing on the porch holding a bunch of flowers, the coldness in her cracked.

She was still angry. Harper hadn't forgiven Lauren, and she didn't know if she would ever be able to. The spying with the phone might be something that Harper could get over, but she couldn't get over the assumptions that had led to it. Of course she had never forgotten that Lauren was a movie star with a lot of money, but she had never considered them as anything other than equal. Harper had never accepted anything from Lauren that she didn't give in return. If they went anywhere, they took turns paying, or bringing food. She didn't think that anyone had insulted her the way Lauren had earlier that day.

Now Lauren was here, and Harper felt as ridiculously happy to see her as she always did. Lauren reached forward and squeezed her hand, apologizing with her eyes. Harper knew they should talk, but her dad was calling out from the kitchen. He was more excited than Harper had seen him in a while. He had even gotten up from his armchair and helped her with getting dinner ready, clumsily chopping onions and setting the table.

"Is that our guest?" he called.

"Yes, Dad," Harper replied. She still hadn't said a word to Lauren. "Come on in."

Lauren followed her down the hall and into the kitchen, where her dad was standing expectantly. He had dressed in one of his few good shirts, his hair still wet from the shower, freshly parted and combed.

"Dad this is Lauren. Lauren, this is my dad."

"You can call me Henry. I'm glad you could come after all." Her dad shook Lauren's hand, putting one of his palms over their joined ones and patting her. Harper felt Lauren's eyes on her, questioning and wondering what kind of story she'd told him to explain. When Lauren took her hand away, she adjusted her clothes and cleared her throat. Despite her anger, it melted her a little to see Lauren looking so eager to please.

"I'm glad too," Lauren said. "It's wonderful to meet you."

Harper turned around to see Tommy hovering in the doorway. "Come here, Tommy. This is Lauren, Lauren this is Tommy."

"Pleasure to meet you." Tommy puffed his chest out, towering over Lauren. Harper watched him trying to act manly and it melted her heart. He still had a lot of growing up to do but it was at times like this that she realized he wasn't far from being an adult.

"I apologize in advance for his questions," said Harper, smiling. "He's always bugging me about the movie. He's been getting some street cred at school because of it."

"Shut up."

"I'll be happy to answer your questions, Tommy," said Lauren. "It's very nice to meet you too."

"Do you think we could get a selfie?"

Harper was horrified. "Tommy! I told you not to ask her for anything like that."

Lauren waved Harper's concern off, smiling into the camera with an arm around Tommy's shoulders. Harper pushed back tears at the sight of Tommy's beaming face. He'd been through a lot for someone so young, and it meant a lot that Lauren was being this sweet with him.

When they sat down to dinner, Harper listened quietly while her dad and Tommy peppered Lauren with questions. Tommy was a movie buff, so he asked her a lot of questions about directors she had worked with. When Lauren casually told him insider gossip about them, Harper could see him storing up the information, no doubt desperate to pass it on to his friends. The only time Harper needed to intervene was when her dad started gently grilling Lauren about her family. He wanted to know who her parents were and what they did, and he wanted to hear all about where she was from. When Harper changed the subject, Lauren shot her a grateful look.

Her dad sipped at his whiskey all night like he always did, but at least he wasn't drunk. He looked pleased when Lauren agreed to join him in a drink and even more pleased when she had several. They were getting along well, Lauren talking with him about the house and about the cars he still loved working on. Every now and then, Lauren would glance at Harper and a sad look would play over her face. Harper knew that Lauren was seeking reassurance from her, but she couldn't bring herself to give it.

On the surface, the night was a success. Her brother and father were enjoying themselves and everyone got along better than she would have hoped. But Harper wasn't happy. When she had first started making plans to surprise Lauren with the invitation, she hadn't imagined that the situation between them would be so uncertain. It would have been better to keep it off the table like she wanted, but she had relented at the last minute when she'd gotten Lauren's message. Going ahead with it was an exercise in denial. It was play-acting at a relationship, marking milestones in something they both knew was going to have to end soon. You weren't supposed to introduce someone to your family right before you parted ways. The thought brought a lump to her throat. She picked up her drink and sipped it, drumming her fingers on the side.

Lauren must have picked up on her mood because she discreetly put her hand on Harper's knee under the table, stroking it gently. Harper flinched not because it was unwanted, but because of the strong reaction she always had when Lauren touched her. Harper caught her hand and held her fingers for a moment.

After dessert, Lauren pushed back her chair. "I've had such a nice night. Thank you all so much. I hope you won't mind if I leave my car here, and come back for it tomorrow? I've had a little too much whiskey to drive."

"Well, Harper and I would be happy to walk you home, but wouldn't you rather stay here?" her dad asked. "I assumed you would sleep over."

"Thank you so much, but I really should be going," Lauren said, looking hopefully at Harper.

"I insist. We'd love to have you stay," he said. Harper watched while he walked over and put his hands on Lauren's shoulders. The whole time she had been watching like a bystander who had nothing to do with any of this. Even now she kept it up, feeling only mild curiosity about what her dad was going to say. "You're always welcome here."

"Thanks, that's very kind of you."

"Well, I mean it. Harper's had a rough few years, having to look after everyone. Even having to live here I think, sometimes," he said, holding up a hand when Harper tried to protest. "No honey, it's true. You're like your mom—you're a city girl. Anyway, Harper's been happier lately, being with you. I want to thank you for that."

He was too drunk to notice the way Lauren's eyes widened subtly in surprise, but Harper saw it. She wished he hadn't said anything. It was only going to create more problems, given Lauren's paranoia about people finding out about them. Her dad had teased her mercilessly over the past few weeks about her secret girlfriend and Harper had continually brushed him off. She hadn't imagined that he would give a speech like that.

At last, he clapped Lauren on the shoulders again and announced that he was going to turn in. Tommy said the same, with a smirk on his face that Harper wanted to slap off. She was going to have to talk to him about not going around school saying anything about what her dad had just implied. Tommy usually showed good sense but you never knew. He was still a teenage boy.

Harper nodded toward her room and Lauren followed her in. She turned on some quiet music because of the possibility that Tommy might try to eavesdrop.

"I don't suppose you'll believe me if I tell you I haven't told Dad anything?" Harper said. "He's said things before and I've always shot him down, so he doesn't know anything for sure. He's just guessing."

Lauren sat down on the bed and looked up at her. "Of course I believe you. I was just surprised, but I don't mind. He's your dad; it would be okay to tell him. I thought what he said was very nice."

"If you say so," Harper said.

Lauren rubbed her palms on her jeans. "I'm sorry I drank that whiskey and couldn't go home. I didn't mean to put you in an awkward position. I was nervous tonight. But I had a lovely time. Thank you for letting me come here."

"It's okay," Harper said, sighing. She wanted to go to sleep, if only to escape all of this. It was too confusing.

"Can you sit next to me? I want to talk to you about something." Despite her anger and disappointment, Harper once again could not say no. She sat down carefully on the bed. She hated that being this close to Lauren made her forget how tired she was. She could smell Lauren's hair and wanted to grab on to it and kiss her in spite of everything.

Lauren took her hand. "I wanted to come over because I did a lot of thinking today. You were right when you said I was reluctant to get involved with you. Somehow I've never been able to help myself."

"Me neither," Harper said. She had no idea where Lauren's words were leading. But when she looked into Lauren's blue eyes she forgot herself, she forgot everything.

"I want to be with you. I want us to make this work. I've wanted that for a while, but I've been scared that you wouldn't want it too." Lauren said it and then held her breath.

Harper could feel an ache in her chest. "Lauren," she started, her voice full of the sense of the hopelessness that she felt.

"Don't," Lauren whispered. "I just needed to try. But I can't bear to hear you say it."

"Please don't be upset," Harper said.

Lauren stared at her, then stood up and paced the room for a second. Harper understood that she needed a moment to escape, even when she couldn't go anywhere. Lauren put her hands behind her head and then sat back down again, folding into herself. "Have I made you fall out of love with me that quickly? That has to be some sort of a record."

"I meant it when I said that I love you. But look at what happened this morning. I can't live in this sort of secrecy. It's been beautiful, and it will always be special to me, but there's too much working against us."

"If that's the only reason, then I'll leave acting, I'll give it up," Lauren said. "I was thinking today about how insecure I always act and how much I mess things up. I've turned into this stunted person who can't live a normal life. I can focus on my writing career. I've got enough money to leave acting."

"What? Lauren, you can't just quit. You don't really mean that. You can't do that for someone else, you'd have to do it for you." As much as it thrilled her to hear that Lauren would even consider it, she knew that it would only cause resentment in the end.

"That's what I'm saying though. You've just helped bring all of this to a head. I haven't been happy for a long time. Maybe that's what all of this has been leading to."

"Maybe so, but you need to work that out on your own time. I would never ask you to do that," Harper said firmly. "And Lauren, I hate to say this but that's not our only problem. I think you must know that. You couldn't very well pick up your whole life and move here, could you?"

Lauren looked down at her hands, raised one up, and started chewing on a fingernail. "And I can't ask you to move away from your family either. Especially after tonight, seeing you all together. I know you've had your problems and stuff, but you are a really tight family."

"We are." Harper couldn't even allow herself to think about the possibility of leaving her dad and Tommy behind. Being there for them was one of the most important things in the world for her. Tommy needed to have at least one responsible adult in the house and her father, for all his good qualities, just couldn't be that for him right now. "I hadn't told you this, but Sal actually offered me a job. It's in LA and not New York, but he offered me a lot of money."

"I knew he was thinking about it. You turned him down?"

Harper nodded. "I couldn't even really consider it."

"So it's really impossible then, isn't it?" Lauren said, but Harper got the sense that she was hoping to be contradicted.

"I wish that it weren't," Harper said. "But yes, it is impossible. I'm sorry."

"Can we stop pretending?" Lauren asked, looking into her eyes. Harper felt so lost in that gaze again. It took her a moment to even register what Lauren had said.

"Pretending?"

"We've been going along like everything is fine, and I've been pretending this whole time that I was okay with this being a short-term thing. This isn't just some cute holiday romance thing for me. I haven't been okay with that at all."

Lauren's voice caught on that last sentence. Maybe it had something to do with the fact that Lauren was an actress, but she was good at hiding her feelings. Although Harper often caught Lauren staring at her with expressions she didn't understand, she hadn't realized that this was the substance of so many of her thoughts.

She grabbed Lauren's hand and squeezed it. "That's not what it's been for me either."

"I'll never forget about this. Do you get that?" Lauren said.

Harper answered with a kiss. She put her arms around Lauren and let herself fall into it. It didn't take long for the kiss to turn into something more, and she didn't want to stop it. It might make things even more complicated but with Lauren grasping at her, her beautiful body so warm and close, there was no question that Harper was going to sink into her and take what Lauren was so eager to give her. Harper clung to Lauren, trying to be quiet so that they would not be heard through the thin walls.

By now they had learned very well what the other person liked, knew how to drive one another crazy. There was something different about it this time, the fight they'd had stoking the passion between them.

Harper didn't know how much more of this they would have. Burying herself in Lauren, she tried to forget.

CHAPTER NINETEEN

As the production wound down, Harper watched the dismantling of everything with less interest than she had watched it come together. It was creation in the reverse, and it depressed her. All of her co-workers looked like they were ready to be done with the movie, Sal more than anybody. While they wrapped things up, the crew talked about what they would do when they got home, whether they were taking a break or if they had another job lined up. Because of the atmosphere of the set, which had felt like its own little universe so much of the time, she had forgotten how many of her colleagues had families they were missing. They all wanted to get back to their lives; she was the only person here who had not really had to leave hers.

There would be no homecoming for her. Going back to her regular job would be a big change. It all seemed so boring now, the endless routine of calling orders, carrying plates, counting tips. For the last eighteen months, she knew she must start to think about direction, about taking the pause off her life. That voice in the back of her head got louder and louder as this chapter came toward its end.

One of the best things about this last week was that she and Lauren dropped the charade of only being friends around Harper's family. Harper had stopped sneaking out of her window. Instead she just called out a hasty good-bye to whoever was around when she left to go to the cottage each night. She rushed out as soon as she had cooked dinner or done the laundry. Sometimes, she wouldn't even bother with those things. Tommy and her father even started picking up after themselves more. They were uncharacteristically considerate about the fact that she didn't want to be at home too much this week.

Lauren had started to set things back in their places at the cottage, and everything looked sparkling clean. She was working on getting the place ready to hand in the keys and leave it behind. It was so strange to think that someone else would be sleeping in the bed soon, that it wouldn't be their special place anymore. Harper knew she was never going to be able to walk past this street again without thinking about Lauren.

They arranged to go to the wrap party together. It was all so close to being done that it didn't seem to matter how much they were seen together. The party was being held at The Tavern. While they ate dinner, Harper held Lauren's hand under the table. She resented spending this time with other people. She would much rather that they were alone.

After dinner, Sal stood up and clinked a spoon on his glass. Slowly the chatter in the room quieted down. "Okay everyone. Hopefully I'll see some of your faces at the Oscar parties after we've won Best Picture."

The room let out a collective groan together, and Sal clinked his spoon again to quiet the crowd. "Okay, let's try that again. I hope I will see you at the premiere, and that this perfectly adequate movie makes us all a boatload of money. Or more specifically, makes me a lot of money." He waited while people clapped and roared. "I know that my particular brand of eccentricity, which, let's face it, comes with the curse of frustrated genius, can be hard to work with. But I want you all to know that I appreciate that you not only put up with me, you work really hard for me." Sal listed off a large number of people, naming what must be almost everyone who had worked on the movie. When he mentioned Harper, she felt Lauren's eyes on her.

"And now I've saved the best for last. Thank you to Lauren. Maybe the only person who nobody here can say a bad word about. You are kind, you have integrity and talent, and I hope I get to make a million more movies with you."

The crowd erupted into cheers. Lauren gave a bashful, grateful wave to the room. Someone suggested that she give a speech. Sal placed the microphone in front of her. She pushed it off immediately, but not before it caught her saying "Not a chance." They all laughed and Sal raised a toast, which everyone enthusiastically took part in.

As soon as the room started to move on from the speech, Harper realized that she was at risk of crying. For everyone else here this was just a party like any other industry party. They could make flippant jokes and know that they would go on to many other jobs and experiences not so different from this one. Harper slipped away while someone was congratulating Lauren on her work and went to the bathroom.

Harper stood before the mirror and appraised herself to see how well she was holding herself together. Her eyes were only a little wet, hopefully not enough for anyone to notice. Taking some tissue and wiping them dry, she fixed up her eyeliner. Then she breathed in as deeply as she could. She told herself that she had made her choices. There was no point wishing that things were different. Having a love affair with a Hollywood actress had always been an unlikely and strange scenario. It was ending, and life was returning to its natural order. It was okay to mourn it, but it was foolish to let it take over.

While she looked in the mirror, Lauren appeared in the bathroom doorway. Harper turned and smiled at her.

"Are you okay?" Lauren asked.

Harper leaned back against the sink and nodded.

Lauren approached her and put a hand on her cheek. "We can go soon."

Harper drew her shoulders up defensively. She didn't want to give the impression that she wasn't able to handle this, not after she had put so much energy into being practical and sensible. "We just got here."

"I don't care about any of this. I just want to spend time with you. Just the two of us."

Harper smiled. "Only a little longer, then."

Harper had lost count of how many nights she had spent at the cottage, but she went back there tonight with a nervous excitement. Something had unlocked inside of her in front of the mirror, an awareness of exactly what she was losing, and now she didn't know how to act. It felt unnatural to behave as though nothing was wrong, but she didn't want to initiate another conversation about the situation they were in either. She had been the one to tell Lauren once and for all that they needed to be pragmatic. It would be unfair to confuse things by saying anything different about it now.

They started kissing the moment they were inside. Lauren pushed her up against the door as soon as it was closed. Harper smiled into her mouth at the familiarity of it.

"You like doing that," Harper said when they came up for breath.

"What?" Lauren said, kissing her neck.

"Jumping on me as soon as we're alone. I'm not complaining by the way."

They worked their way down the hall. When they got closer to the bedroom, Lauren made her turn so that she could cover her eyes.

"I've got a surprise for you," she said, guiding Harper forward toward the bed.

"Oh, you are so cheesy," Harper said when Lauren uncovered her eyes. There were candles on the nightstands and rose petals scattered over the bed.

"You love that about me," Lauren replied. "I wanted to make it special."

Harper caught the vulnerability in her tone. "What's that?" Harper asked as she came closer to the bed. There was a black jewelry box in the middle of the quilt.

"Don't worry, I'm not proposing. I just wanted to get you something." Lauren walked over and sat down, patting the space beside her. "Come here?"

Harper approached and joined her on the bed. Lauren took out the ring and slipped it on a finger on Harper's right hand. It was a simple silver band, nothing too showy and exactly to her taste.

"Thank you," Harper said, kissing her. "I wish I'd gotten something for you too. I'm sorry."

"Don't be sorry. I just wanted you to have something to remember me by."

"Like I could forget you," Harper said, shaking her head and putting her arms around Lauren. "It's perfect."

As they moved onto the bed, they each knew that it must be the last time. Harper could feel it, the sense that they were each trying to make it all count, trying to make the best memories they could. They made love for hours, touching one another in a kind of worship.

When it was over at last she felt a surge of emotion, the afterglow leaving her vulnerable to the tears she'd been suppressing for the last few hours. Harper tried to hide them at first, her face turned away from Lauren in the darkness.

"Don't cry, Harper," Lauren said softly, her fingers trailing over Harper's face to confirm what she was already sure of.

"I miss you so much already. I don't want you to go," Harper said through her tears.

Lauren grabbed Harper and held her tight. They lay like that, fused together.

"I don't want to say good-bye to you either," Lauren said after a long time.

"Me neither. Let's not say good-bye. Let's just do that thing where we pretend we're not and say like, see you later. Dad and I used to do that when I was going back to the city after a visit. I know it's silly, but it helps."

"I can do that. I think it will make it feel a little less hard."

They fell into an exhausted sleep for a couple of hours. When the morning came, Harper was the first to wake up. It was dawn and she could hear the sounds of birds chirping. She lay on her side and watched Lauren sleep for a few minutes, observing the rise and fall of her chest and the way her hands curled over her stomach protectively. Her face looked peaceful, free of the hurt she had seen on it a couple of times the night before. Harper had never felt this strongly about a person in her life. She would do anything to make sure that the pain never reappeared. If their situation were any less impossible, she knew that she would happily wake up to look at that face every day.

They had talked out how this morning was going to play out. When Lauren woke up, they set about putting their plan in motion, not talking very much at first. They were both tired. Harper took a long shower to wake herself up. Anxiety about their parting was slowly building up. She kept breathing deeply, trying to shake it off. This was hard for Lauren too, and Harper wanted to be strong for her.

Harper helped with finishing up packing the last of Lauren's things and loading them into the car. It was strange to see the way Lauren's whole life for the past few months could be squeezed into a few cases. Before Harper clipped Chester onto the seat belt, she cuddled him for a long time. She had become attached to his presence, and hadn't known she could care so much about an animal. It was hard to imagine that they would have gotten together without him. Chester had given them an excuse to talk to one another before they had known how.

When the two of them were about to walk out the door, Harper put her hand on Lauren's arm. "Wait."

"What did I forget?" Lauren asked, looking around the room.

"We're not going to be able to kiss good-bye at the airport, so…" Harper raised her eyebrows.

"Oh," Lauren said. She stood before Harper, who pulled her closer by the hips. They must have kissed a thousand times by now, but the sight of Lauren coming near to her still gave her tingles. They lingered over the kiss, Lauren putting her hands on Harper's waist and keeping her close. When they pulled away, they were both breathing rapidly.

Harper looked down at her watch. She was trying to calculate whether they had time for more, and was disappointed to see that they really had to go now. Drawing out their good-byes would just make it worse anyway. "Well, let's hit the road shall we?"

It was a long drive to the airport, and they spent most of the trip in silence. Harper looked out of the window. She couldn't bear the thought of making small talk at a time like this. Instead, she dug her fingernails into the palm of her hand and leaned her forehead against the glass. She wanted to say something important, something with meaning, but couldn't think of the right thing. The sensation was so uncomfortable, the two of them going about the business of leaving one another without a word. It made her want to do something dramatic, to scream or shout, but she knew she never would.

At last, with the rental car returned and the baggage checked, they were alone at the gate with a polite distance between them. Lauren held her hands stiffly at her sides.

"Well, so. I'll see you later?" Lauren said, trying to smile.

"See you later," Harper replied. Lauren leaned in and hugged her, then turned and walked away. The fact that she didn't look over her shoulder might have hurt, if Harper hadn't been able to see the unsteadiness in her gait.

Harper covered her mouth. Her stomach churned. The bus trip home now seemed as though it required enormous effort, because it meant interacting with people. Harper had insisted on coming to the airport with Lauren rather than drive her own car, but now she wished she had the privacy a vehicle would have afforded her. Harper slipped into one of the backseats on the bus and blankly watched the same things she had seen on the way over reverse themselves.

It was unthinkable that she had let it all happen the way it had. Why couldn't she have been braver? Why hadn't she accepted the idea that they should try, like Lauren suggested?

At the time, she told herself that she was being realistic because Lauren couldn't or wouldn't be. She hadn't been able to see the sense in talking about something that could never become a reality. That now struck her as cowardice. Lauren was the brave one, wanting to risk some of herself, and Harper was foolish. At some point, she had fallen into a rut and lost any sense of imagination about a different type of life. Lauren deserved better than her.

Harper had to remind herself that no real tragedy had occurred. Lauren was still out there; she was alive and well. Right now, she would be sitting on a plane. Maybe she was looking out the window down at the clouds, or reading the newspaper.

Harper could tell herself that there had been no catastrophe, but she did not believe it. They had lost one another.

CHAPTER TWENTY

As soon as she got on the plane, Lauren put on her armor. Learning how to detach from her emotions had helped her survive, a skill that she had developed as a child. There was a danger that if she began to let herself feel she would start crying and wouldn't be able to stop. Falling apart was not something she could afford. There was work to do, and soon.

Talking to the press meant trying to be articulate but not *too* clever, warm but not desperate, bubbly yet genuine. It meant being asked the same questions over and over and trying to act like the answer was fresh each time. It was tiring, especially for someone who was full of as many secrets as she was. No matter how well she thought she performed, there was always the chance that something she said would cause a minor scandal.

At least she would be in New York for a while. Franklin, her publicist, had hired a hotel room where the interviews would be conducted, which meant that she could go home at the end of each day. Being at home with all of her things around her might give her a sense of normalcy. The idea that she could be happy without Harper was unthinkable. Still, she had to believe that if she kept going through the motions she could return to the normal rhythms of life and eventually feel okay again.

When she walked through the door of her apartment, it was quiet and stuffy in a way that made her sigh. It felt so much less like home than the cottage had. She unpacked and watered the plants that Melinda had kept alive for her, then followed Chester around while he sniffed things and reacquainted himself with the space.

A lump came to her throat when she checked her phone and saw that Harper had sent her a text message. It was short, just two kisses and no words. After a long period of deliberation, she sent back the same thing. Lauren wanted to say that she missed her, or that she loved her, but couldn't see how it would help the situation.

A friend asked her to go out to dinner so he could welcome her home, but she told him that she was too tired from traveling. If she went, she would spend the whole night talking about Harper. Nobody knew that she had been seeing someone and she wasn't ready to talk about it. Instead, Lauren ordered Chinese food and turned on the television, zoning out.

She went to bed early, the long empty night stretching out ahead of her. When she felt sad or anxious, sleep was the first thing to suffer. It was so weird being back in her own bed, alone. When she started to drift off, she snapped awake only to look around and see a room that had become unfamiliar to her. The city was loud outside her window. She had ceased to notice the noise a long time ago but spending months away had sharpened her senses again.

Lauren reached out and looked at her phone to see if Harper had called, even though she would have heard it if she had. Lauren wondered if she should make contact, just to say good night and see how she was doing. Her pride stopped her because she didn't think she could take it if Harper was anything less than ecstatic to hear from her. They hadn't even discussed how they were going to navigate this part. Lauren had wanted to know but hadn't wanted to try and talk about it. She had put herself out there enough when she had talked to Harper about trying to continue the relationship, so she didn't want to risk rejection again.

At last, she drifted off. When she woke up she knew she had just left a dream about Harper. She couldn't remember much about the content of it but it left her with a deep sense of longing. The vision of red hair and brown eyes lingered while she rose and got ready to start her day.

Each outfit she tried on looked wrong. Whatever she wore would be described in every article that was written about today's interviews, and there would be filmed content too. One couldn't really go wrong with black. Given that it perfectly reflected her mood she decided to go with it. She pulled on a black sleeveless button-up top and her best pair of designer jeans, then hastily added some accessories so it wouldn't look too plain.

A car picked her up and took her uptown to the hotel. When she got there, the room was buzzing with the trinity of her manager, publicist and her assistant. She was glad to see Melinda at least, who gave her a warm hug and told her in a genuine way that she looked good. Celia, her manager, and Franklin were not happy as they looked her up and down when she came in. Celia muttered that she should have worn a skirt instead of jeans. A surge of anger went up Lauren's spine. It wasn't unusual for them to talk about her as though she couldn't hear them perfectly well, but after time away from them, it bothered her more.

Lauren asked for herbal tea and sat while hair and makeup people buzzed around her. Franklin gave her a list of talking points about the movie she was promoting. She looked them over resentfully, thinking about how ridiculous it was that she was told what opinions she was allowed to express. Before she had left for Texas, she had seen an early cut of *Empty Nests*. They had a battle on their hands trying to sell this one, so maybe it was a good thing that she was being fed her lines. It had been a promising script, but it was badly watered down and had changed beyond recognition. Lauren gritted her teeth and started memorizing what she was supposed to say.

It was depressing to think that in the future she would have to promote *Texas Twist*. How would she ever be able to talk about it as though it was just another movie? It would always be the vehicle that took her to Harper. The thought of being told to drop silly hints about her supposed relationship with Josh made her feel sick.

Thankfully, the first reporter to come in was Jack Griggs, a friendly guy from one of the more prestigious magazines. Lauren was aware that her publicist carefully coordinated the order of her interviews to get a better performance from her. Jack's presence meant that she probably wouldn't like the next person who walked through the door. Jack stuck to questions about her work, he knew what he was talking about, and he pretty much wrote what she expected that he would. They had a pleasant and warm interview. Lauren felt temporarily buoyed.

As predicted, the next interview was with someone she couldn't stand—Maria Standforth. From the moment they met when Lauren was a rising star, Maria had rubbed her the wrong way. She always put herself into the story as much as possible. Years ago Maria had written a nasty profile about Lauren that made her sound vacuous and insecure. Despite the fact that Franklin explicitly briefed her every single time about the no personal questions rule, Maria never failed to push the boundaries. Lauren wanted to refuse her further interviews but Franklin insisted that Maria was too powerful to cut out.

The way Maria shook her hand and smiled that plastic grin set Lauren's teeth on edge. On any other day, Lauren would have found her only mildly irritating, but she had never felt as sensitive as she did today. Her sadness was so close to the surface. It occurred to her that it was people like Maria who were responsible for some of her problems. They helped to rob her of courage, rendering her ashamed and afraid.

At first, the questions were innocuous. Maria was smart enough to know to start out that way. But it didn't take long for her to start slipping in the type of questions Lauren hated. Could Lauren relate to her working-class character, and had she come from a similar background? Then she stepped back by asking what it was like working with the little girl who played her daughter. Two steps forward with the question of whether Lauren was looking forward to marriage and kids of her own, and when was she going to start a family anyway? That one earned her a subtle head shake from Franklin. When Maria asked whether her character's family shared traits with Lauren's, Lauren cut her off and asked for a glass of water.

Lauren didn't say a word while she waited for Melinda to bring her a glass of water, and Maria didn't either. She wasn't bothering to put on a polite façade with this woman.

The water did nothing to cool her temper, though. The more she thought about it, the more she couldn't bear Maria's entitled attitude. It reminded her of every photographer that had ever shoved a camera in her face while she walked through the airport. It brought to mind every time someone thought they had the right to take things from her that she had never intended to offer. It recalled every person that claimed she was asking to have her privacy violated by becoming an actor in the first place.

Lauren looked at Maria with open hostility. The moment stretched out awkwardly. She mentally dared the journalist to ask her another stupid question to see what would happen. Maria stood her ground and looked back at her with a bemused expression that she guessed was supposed to make her feel ashamed of herself.

"Why do you guard your private life so closely? What are you hiding?" Maria suddenly blurted out. Lauren glared over at Franklin. She was waiting for a rescue but he'd gone uncharacteristically quiet.

"Excuse me?" Lauren said.

"I'm just wondering why you're so annoyed by simple questions about family. These questions aren't invasive. Everyone has a family. Don't they? You don't talk to your family, do you, and that's why the sensitivity?"

"I'm terminating this interview."

Franklin put up a hand. "Let's take a five-minute break, guys."

"I'm not taking a break, I told you I'm done. I'm finished speaking to her."

Lauren glowered at Maria, who was staring at her. Lauren didn't understand why she was acting surprised, when she had been working hard at getting this sort of reaction. It would give her a nice, juicy story to write about how Lauren was ungrateful and rude.

"Honestly, this is very unprofessional behavior," Maria said. "I think people deserve to know what you're hiding."

"Oh please. I don't need to be lectured about professional standards by a bottom-feeding vulture like you," Lauren snapped. Gasps rippled through the room. She stood up and walked toward the door, holding it open.

Maria had no choice but to do as she was asked, but she glared at Lauren and shook her head in disgust the whole way. Lauren closed the door behind her and then stood for a moment, loosely gripping the knob. It was difficult for her to believe that she had just acted like that, but she couldn't deny that it felt good. Lauren took a deep breath. Now that she didn't have Harper, there was nothing important left for her to lose.

Lauren turned around. "I'll do the rest of today's interviews and tomorrow's too. I'm not stupid; I know what my obligations are. But Franklin, Celia? I'm letting you both go. You've been giving me bad advice."

Franklin held out his hands, looking at Celia then back at Lauren in exasperation. Lauren could imagine exactly what he was thinking. That she was throwing a childish hissy fit, that she was just another neurotic client on a power trip. The fact that Lauren had independent thoughts and feelings was an inconvenience to him.

"Lauren, if you want me to apologize for bringing her in here then fine, I will," he said. "We know you don't like her. I'll cut her off like you've been wanting me to. Okay?"

"Nope," Lauren replied. "That's not enough. Neither of you have never listened to me. All you do is tell me what I should think, what I should want. I want to work with people who respect my opinion."

"Darling, you're obviously tired," Celia said. "You know Franklin and I think the world of you. We're here to handle the business side of things so you don't have to worry about it. But if it's what you want, we'll consult you more. Let's sit down and have a meeting about it tomorrow, when you're feeling a bit fresher."

It only strengthened her resolve. They were acting like she was a spooked animal, something they just needed to wrangle.

"Thank you for offering to consult me. But I pay you and I'm your boss, so it's actually the least you could do. I want to go in another direction. That's the end of the discussion. It must be time to bring in the next interview."

Lauren spent the rest of the day doubling her efforts to be charming and co-operative. She wasn't sure how much she cared about her career at this point, but it was a strategic move. If Maria wrote an ugly article about her, she wanted it to be drowned out by positive ones, if only so that Maria wouldn't win by damaging her reputation.

It was a lonely day. Some of the people in the room were kind toward her, like Melinda, but there was nobody here she could really talk to.

Harper would understand, and she would encourage her to fight. Lauren would give anything to have Harper by her side.

CHAPTER TWENTY-ONE

Harper woke up with the same gnawing emptiness in her gut that had been there the day before. She had never been the kind of person that had to drag themselves out of bed, but she had to today. Before she rose, she spent half an hour staring at the ceiling and wondering how she was going to deal with this. It hurt so much more than she had thought it would.

At least she had a day off before she had to go back to work at the diner. She packed up a bag with a book, her journal and a thermos. At the last minute she decided she had better eat, so she put some leftover mac and cheese she made for her brother in a container. It occurred to her that she hadn't eaten dinner the night before.

When she got to the lake, she sat and looked out over the water. She wondered how many times she had stared out at the same view with Lauren by her side. The tears came and Harper didn't fight them. She let the emotions of the last few weeks overwhelm her. This was why she had to come here, because she had known this was going to happen sooner or later, and she needed to be alone when it did. Harper lay back on her picnic blanket and put her arm over her face. It had been a long time since she had cried like this. It felt like a heavy weight had been laid on her chest, the pain physical.

After a while, she sat up and wiped her face with her sleeve. The silver ring Lauren gave her caught the light and she touched it, running her finger over the metal. Harper was filled with an angry impulse to throw it into the lake. It didn't make sense that she should feel upset with Lauren for leaving, but she was angry nonetheless. Harper took off the ring and felt the weight of it in her palm. When she picked it up again she noticed engraving on the inside. Assuming that it was just a manufacturer's stamp, she turned it to take a closer look, and saw that it was an inscription: *My love, forever.*

It was just like Lauren to do something like that and not even draw her attention to it. How could Lauren say such things and mean them when they had only known each other for a short time? Yet she felt the same way and could not imagine a time when her love might fade away. How could there be a day when Lauren was only a memory, and this ring just didn't mean that much to her anymore? If Harper were to meet someone else, she couldn't exactly go on wearing it. She imagined herself putting the ring away in a drawer, something that she took out now and then and looked at fondly. It was impossible.

This was not her first breakup, if that's what this even was. She had been through enough in her life to know that the saying "time heals all wounds" had some truth in it. There was no way of guessing how long it would take, but she could be sure that the pain would dull and she would be able to go on with her life, albeit with a few new scars. That knowledge was of small comfort to her right now.

On the drive home, she realized that she felt lighter, that her tears had been cleansing. A Springsteen song that Lauren loved came on the radio and she listened to it for a moment, flashing back to a night when Lauren had sung along quietly with the lyrics as they drove to the lake. Harper reached over and pressed the knob to silence the radio.

When she got home, she was shocked by the smell wafting through the house, because it was obvious that somebody had been cooking. Harper couldn't remember the last time anyone else had made a proper dinner. Tommy and her dad both fried themselves bacon and eggs or heated up a TV dinner now and then, but they never sat down to eat together anymore. It had been up to Harper to nag them about it and to try and get her dad interested in food, even though he had been a really good cook once. Harper walked into the dining room to see her dad piling chicken and dumplings onto plates. Her brother was watching him. They were talking and stopped when they realized that she was there.

Her dad wiped his hands on the front of his shirt. "Harper! Glad you made it home in time, I thought I was going to have to try to keep this stuff warm for you for later."

"Yeah," Harper said warily. It wasn't that she was unhappy to see them together like this, but it made her feel like something was up.

"Well sit down and let's eat then," her dad said, as though he cooked for the family all of the time.

"Okay," Harper said. Her appetite hadn't been great today but it returned in full force thanks to the mouth-watering smell. They room filled with the sounds of clinking knives and forks and chewing mouths.

"So, Lauren went back home yesterday?" her dad asked.

"Yep," Harper said, her fork slowing as it returned to her plate. She pushed a piece of chicken around on its surface, trailing it through broth.

"How did you guys leave it then?"

Harper glanced at her brother, who was staring at her. Of course they knew, and she'd known that they knew, but she had made it clear that she didn't want to talk about it.

Harper shrugged. "She has work, I have work. Not much we can do about that."

"But you would keep seeing her if you could, right? Have you made plans to see each other again?" he pressed.

"Dad, thanks for your concern, but I don't want to talk about it."

Tommy was looking awkwardly down into his dinner. Harper ate faster, hoping to get away from the table as soon as possible. She looked over and realized that her dad didn't have a drink sitting by his plate. Lauren looked up into his clear eyes. By now he usually didn't get drunk enough to slur his words or stumble, but she could always tell by his eyes.

Her dad nodded a couple of times uncomfortably, and Harper felt guilty for her evasiveness. He was obviously trying.

"This dinner is delicious, Dad. It's real good to taste your cooking again." Harper smiled at him.

He grinned back at her, pleased. "I was just glad to find out I hadn't forgotten how. I showed Tommy how I do it too. I'm going to teach him how to cook."

Harper looked across at Tommy. "Really?"

"I told him, a man should know how to cook. A man should know how to do everything for himself."

Neither of them had ever shown much interest in helping her out. Harper didn't mean to look skeptical, but they must have been able to see it on her face.

"Dad says I need to start doing more around the house," Tommy added.

"That would be great," Harper said, opting for being gracious instead of saying that it was about time and she was beyond sick of nagging them.

"Now, there's something I've been wanting to tell you kids. I'm going away for a little while. Just a week or two," her dad said.

So that was what this was all about. The out-of-character behavior was just his way of buttering her up for something. She waited patiently for him to come out with the rest of the story. A fearful sliver of herself worried that he might leave and never come back, that he might just finish the process of going away from them. For years he had left inch by inch in spirit, if not in body.

"I'm going into a treatment facility. For the drinking. Gotta dry out," he said.

Harper looked back at him in shock. It was the last thing that she had expected him to say. It was something she had never stopped worrying about, but she had long ago stopped trying to talk to him about it. The last time she suggested that he was drinking too much, they had a huge argument.

"Cool," Tommy said, as though their dad had just said that he was going on a fishing trip.

"When did you decide this?" Harper asked.

"I've been cutting back for a while, but the doc says if I want to stop properly, I need a bit of help. So that's what I'm doing."

"Okay," Harper said. She put down her knife and fork, feeling a lump in her throat.

"Okay. I'm not going until Wednesday. Just wanted to let you know."

"Thank you," Harper said. They returned to their meals and ate in silence, the three of them lost in their separate thoughts.

When her father left, Harper tried to not get her hopes up. She knew that her dad might not finish the treatment, or that he might come home and go right back to drinking again. It was strange not having him in the house, but it was also a relief to not have to come home after work and find him already three sheets to the wind, or walk out to the living room to find him slumped in front of the TV with a drink still in his hand. They didn't discuss it, but Tommy seemed happier too.

Each night after work, Harper watched every movie of Lauren's that she could find. It may not be the healthiest way to deal with her grief, she knew that, but she did it anyway. Until recently, *Edge of the Sea* was the only movie of Lauren's that she had ever seen. It was comforting to Harper to see her face, though sometimes it made missing her even more painful. She drew the line at buying magazines to read about Lauren, although the impulse struck her more than once. The idea of learning about Lauren's movements from a source like that depressed her. Anyway, Lauren hated those magazines. Looking

Lauren up on the Internet was out of the question too, because Lauren had warned her about all of the horrible comments people wrote online. Harper didn't want to see that.

It took a week for her to crack. The urge to call Lauren grew until she couldn't stand it anymore. She told herself that it wasn't a failure on her part that she couldn't stay away. All she needed was a check-in thing, just to hear Lauren's voice. It would be strange to spend all of that time together and then never call to find out how Lauren was doing.

Harper prepared for the call as though it were a job interview or a public speaking engagement. She went over it in her mind, musing over what she should say and how she should say it. When she decided that it was time, she took the cordless phone into her bedroom and shut the door behind her, then lay on the bed and squeezed her eyes shut tight. By the time the phone started ringing in her ear, she wasn't sure what she was most afraid of—that Lauren would answer or that she wouldn't.

CHAPTER TWENTY-TWO

Lauren almost missed the call. She was sitting on the fire escape with her legs dangling out over the street, sipping from a can of beer. Her stereo, pulled up close to the window, blasted out Springsteen. It was time to celebrate.

It had only been a week since she had come home, but with each day, she grew more confident about making the changes that had been such a long time coming. Firing Franklin and Celia started a chain reaction. The day she let them go, she contacted her agent and fired him too, and then signed on with a guy called Chris from a smaller firm with a good reputation. They met for the first time earlier in the day. He was respectful and seemed smart. When she described the kinds of roles she wanted from now on, he reeled off a list of directors, producers and writers he thought they should set their sights on. They showed her that he understood her taste and how much of a different direction she wanted to go in.

It had taken her too long to wrestle back control. Now that she had, she felt amazing.

Her cell was on the window ledge, so she heard it vibrating. Lauren glanced over with no intention of answering it when she saw Harper's name on the display. She scrambled so fast that she kicked her beer can over. When she answered, the music was so loud she couldn't hear anything. She frantically turned down the volume.

"Hello? Harper?"

There was a pause. She thought the line was dead, but then Harper responded. "Hey."

Lauren closed her eyes, flooded with relief at the sound of her voice. During the last week, Harper had remained an invisible presence looking over her shoulder. Lauren imagined Harper watching her and wondered whether she would be proud, and whether she would think Lauren was making the right decisions.

"How are you?" Lauren asked.

"I'm okay. How are you?"

It was a difficult question to answer. The pain of leaving Harper had weighed heavily on her. She had to work very hard to distract herself from thinking of her every minute. She also felt anxious about cutting off staff that had worked for her for years, and yet she was elated too. It had been a roller coaster to say the least.

"I'm okay," she said cautiously. There was a silence on the other end of the line.

"How did the press stuff go?" Harper asked.

"Oh, actually it was a bit of a thing. I fired my manager and publicist."

"You did? I always knew you weren't happy with them, but I didn't know you were thinking about letting them go."

"It was a bit impulsive, I guess. But I'm happy about it. I feel like I did the right thing."

"I'm sure you did."

"I hope so. I've got a new agent and we've been making plans. How has it been back at the diner? You've started right?" Lauren asked, mindful that she was talking too much about herself. She pictured the diner, and felt a strong wave of nostalgia for the red vinyl seats and checked floor.

Harper laughed. It sounded awkward, but Lauren wasn't sure why. "It's okay. It's the same old thing, you know?"

"Well, tell Sue hello from me."

"That will make her day," Harper said.

It was quiet again. Lauren stared down at the street, biting her lip. She had been desperate to talk to Harper for days, but she hadn't expected it to feel stilted like this. They never had trouble thinking of things to say to one another, not recently anyway.

"How are your dad and Tommy?" Lauren asked.

"They're good. Listen, I should go. I just wanted to check in," Harper said.

"Oh. Okay," Lauren replied. "Tell your family hello from me, as well."

"Of course, I'll do that. You take care."

The line clicked and it was silent again. Lauren stared at the screen for a long time. When she scanned back over the conversation, she couldn't figure out what she'd said wrong. It was almost worse than having no contact at all, to hear from Harper and then have her go so quickly. Or had Harper only made the call out of a sense of duty, not really wanting to talk to her in the first place?

Lauren's chest ached with everything left unsaid.

A week ago, she would have tortured herself over the call. She would have let it ruin her afternoon, in fact her whole week, and not done a thing about it. Being separated from Harper made her feel like she had nothing left to lose, and somehow that gave her the strength to start going after what she wanted. Now she could feel the hard beating of her heart and knew that she needed to assert herself, even with Harper.

Lauren pressed the button to call her back. If Harper didn't answer, she would keep pressing it until she did. Harper picked up almost immediately.

"Why did you do that?" Lauren asked.

"Do what?"

"You practically hung up on me. Did I say something to upset you?"

Harper sighed, and took a long time to answer. "No Lauren, of course you didn't."

"Then why?"

"I don't know. It's just hard. It affects me, hearing your voice."

Lauren held her breath for a moment. She knew exactly what Harper meant. "It does for me too."

"Okay. I'm sorry."

"Thank you."

Neither of them spoke for a while, each listening to the other's breath. Lauren looked out across the skyline and wondered what Harper could see from wherever she was sitting. Lauren took a deep breath.

"Well. I just really did want to say hello," Harper tried again. "I'm sorry I made it weird. I was just thinking of you."

"It's okay, Harper. We'll talk again soon?"

"We will," Harper said. "I miss you."

Before Lauren could say it back, the line went dead.

Harper's dad didn't announce that it was time for him to come home; he just returned as quietly as he had left. One day she got home from work and there he was, sitting on the porch smoking a cigarette. A weathered old suitcase was next to him, making it obvious that he hadn't been inside yet. It had only been two weeks but he looked different, bright and clear. His face had lost some of its redness.

"You're home," she said warmly.

Seeing him again took away some of the loneliness. The phone call to Lauren had rattled her, and she had been very off her game in the first place. Harper hadn't called her again since then. Harper didn't like to think that she was jealous of Lauren's success, but hearing about Lauren's career made her feel small. It brought home all over again how very different their lives were. It reminded her that Lauren had a whole life that could never have anything to do with her.

"That I am. I missed you kids." He got up and patted her on the shoulder. There was something shy about the way he spoke to her. Life had gone on in such a straight line for so long that this bump in the road was making things strange.

"I see they didn't cure you of that habit," she joked, pointing to the cigarette clutched between his nicotine-stained fingertips.

"No, no. A person has to have at least one vice."

Harper mused about the fact that Lauren might be hers. "How was it?"

He sat back down, drew on his cigarette, and shrugged. "It was okay. I had to go to a lot of silly meetings and therapy session things but they gave me medication, looked after me. I feel pretty good."

"I'm really glad to hear that, Dad. I'm proud of you for going. I know it can't have been easy for you."

He looked at her, then looked away and stubbed out his smoke. "I wanted to say something to you, but I had to wait to see if I could stick it out first."

Harper didn't think she had ever seen him look so nervous. Scenarios went through her mind, like he might say that he was leaving them. She watched uneasily while he lit another cigarette.

"I haven't been a very good father to you and Tommy since your mom died."

Harper put a hand on his shoulder. Just because it was true, it didn't mean she wanted him to say it or even think it. "Daddy, no."

He held up a hand to silence her. "I haven't. Your mom would be ashamed of me, and that's been a hard thing for me to face up to. But I have now. I want you to know that things are going to be better from here on out. I've got big plans."

"I'm glad to hear it. For you, I mean. What are they?"

"I'm going to get back to work, for one thing. And I'm going to get better about Tommy, make sure he and I both start doing things for ourselves. You've been taking on too much for the family."

"I'm happy to do it, Dad. You guys are the most important thing to me. You know that." She hoped that she hadn't been moping around too much about Lauren and making him think that she resented them.

"I do know that, but I want you to consider getting back to your life. If you need to go back to New York, then I think you should go. You know your uncle would take you back in a heartbeat. That's always been the case."

"Dad, I can't just up and leave like that."

"It wouldn't be doing that and you know it. It's where you're supposed to be, where I think you really want to be. We'll visit, stay in touch just like we did last time. I don't want you to have to worry about us so much."

Harper shook her head. This all felt like it was coming out of the blue. "What's brought all this on?"

"Just had what you'd call an epiphany, I guess. I've seen how happy you were with Lauren. It's made me realize how much you've missed out on for us. I can't believe I let it happen, if you want to know the truth. I need to make it right."

Harper watched the way he was sitting, his back straightening in a show of strength. "We can't think of it that way. I've wanted to be here with you guys," Harper said, her eyes filling with tears.

"I know you have. You're a good girl, you put the family first," he said, putting his arm around her. "But you need to think of yourself, think about settling down and all that. I'd be proud to have a daughter-in-law like Lauren."

Harper rested her head on his shoulder. It wasn't the time to tell him that she had let Lauren go, that there might not be a possibility of a relationship with her. Maybe she should go to New York for her own sake, regardless of whether things worked out with Lauren. It was a lot to consider, a whole world opening up when she had thought that door had been long shut behind her.

"Okay. I'll think about it."

CHAPTER TWENTY-THREE

It was not a difficult decision to make when it came down to it, but it was hard to put it all into motion. As soon as Harper thought about it, she knew that going to New York was the only sensible option. Once that was decided, she could see the steps she needed to take laid out before her. Harper had always been a planner. Calling her uncle should be the first move, to find out if that job really was a sure thing and to see if it was okay for her to stay at his place until she could find an apartment. Then she would have to start thinking about what she would need to take with her, and give notice at the diner. She felt a bit crappy about resigning after her job had been held for all that time, but she knew they would all be happy for her too.

It all sounded simple, almost too easy. Yet she felt paralyzed and afraid to start. There was a piece missing from her plan that she was afraid to approach. It didn't seem fair to let Lauren know about her intention to move to New York, not when she didn't know that it was all going to work out. After their last phone call, she was insecure about their future. It appeared that Lauren had slipped easily back into her regular life, and in fact was thriving. Of course Harper was happy about that, but how did she know that there was a place for her?

Lauren was starting to wonder what she had spent all that time so worried about. Maria's nasty article about her barely made a ripple. It blew over faster than she would have imagined. The firing of her staff made industry papers, but it wasn't that unusual, and nobody outside of the inner circle cared.

Lauren still hadn't hired a new publicist and manager, and she was quite happy to wait. She wanted to make sure that next time she chose those people very carefully. In the meantime, she decided that she wanted to have a meeting with Chris to broach the subject that always ended up becoming an issue and causing her so much stress. He suggested a lunch date but she insisted on meeting him in his office, not wanting to be anyplace where they might be overheard.

When she went to his office, she was edgy. As she stood in the elevator, she stared at herself in the mirrored doors. She looked terrified. Lauren rearranged her expression and forced her body to relax. She told herself that she had made the choice to hire Chris, and that if she didn't like what he had to say, she was prepared to fire him just as quickly. Nobody was ever going to make her feel powerless again.

Chris greeted her warmly when she came in and asked his secretary to get her a bottle of water. He slid a script across to her. "This came across my desk and I'd love to put you forward for it. I'm sure you're already on their list, but if you like it I'll make some calls."

Lauren picked it up and looked at the title, then nervously thumbed through the pages. She saw the words but couldn't take any of it in. "Thanks. I'll check it out later, but I actually wanted to talk to you about something more general. Like, about my career direction and image and all that."

He looked across at her, and Lauren saw him clock her nervousness. He waited patiently for her to speak.

"I've had issues in the past with this, so it's the only reason I'm bringing it up."

"Of course. It's good to get things on the table, I'm always ready to learn from the last person's mistakes," he prompted, smiling at her.

"Okay, well, I wanted to talk about the fact that I'm gay," Lauren said, fumbling her words. Chris didn't react at all, except to smile at her.

"Me too. Thanks for letting me know."

"And I don't plan on making any announcements, but I'd like to live a little more openly at least," she said, encouraged by his relaxed attitude. She was used to concern about her and her career, even from other gay people. When he didn't say anything, she kept talking. "I don't want it to affect the roles that I take. I've often been pushed into more romantic-style movies, and I think I want to move toward more dramatic stuff. That way, if it ever comes out it might not matter as much."

"Okay, I understand. I think you're more than capable of more challenging work, for what it's worth. You want to stop having beards, right? I don't think that's going to make such a big difference."

"Do you really think that?"

Chris shrugged. "Sure. I'm not your publicist, but can't they just not have you say anything either way? People can speculate, but you've got a good solid body of work behind you. That's not all just going to go away overnight just because you don't have a boyfriend."

"Well. I think we're on the same page," Lauren said. He was handling this in such a low-key way that she almost felt silly for bringing it up.

"I'm excited to be working together," he said. He leaned over and shook her hand.

"Thank you," Lauren said.

The day Harper left Texas for the second time, her dad had to be dragged kicking and screaming from under a car to give her a ride to the airport. He kept insisting that they had plenty of time, but Harper knew it was just his way of stalling. Despite the fact that he was giving her all the support he could, and in fact was basically pushing her out the door, he had a lot of trouble with good-byes. For the last week he had been spending most of his time working on his truck, getting ready to start at his old job again. He was the best mechanic in town when he wasn't drinking, and everybody knew it.

Finally, she was able to separate him from his pride and joy for long enough to help her take her suitcases out to the car. She had packed light, knowing that she would need to go shopping for new work clothes. Furniture and larger items were going to stay here until she could get her own place and have it all shipped out. Tommy had said that he was too busy to see her off, but at the last moment he slid wordlessly into the backseat, and the three of them set out for the airport. Her dad turned the radio on to his favorite country station and Harper smiled when Tommy groaned from the backseat. She glanced back at him and watched him for a second while he played on his phone. Their eyes met, and he stuck his tongue out at her.

Harper looked forward and made a rude gesture at him over her shoulder, which she knew would make him laugh. It was easier than thinking about other times that they had made this trip together, and about the fact that there was an important person missing. It shouldn't be Harper sitting in the front seat. At least now she would be making some really good new memories. Though she would never stop mourning the missing piece of their family, she was reassured that her dad and Tommy were going to be okay without her.

When they got to the airport, her father insisted on walking her to the gate. Harper felt herself welling up at the way he stood there stiffly. She knew him well enough to know that he was really struggling. In the end, he just patted her on the shoulder and turned around. Tommy tried to do the same, but he was still skinny and slight enough that she could force a hug on him. When she got on the plane, she was struck by a feeling of incredible lightness through the sadness of leaving them. This was right.

Lauren was spending the afternoon walking Chester around the city streets. It had been easy to forget how much she had missed this place, and she was enjoying reacquainting herself with it. She stopped and bought a hot dog and fed most of it to Chester, then walked into the park. It was a beautiful sunny day today and she was feeling good. Though she missed Harper more than she could bear at times, she tried to appreciate the good times when they came.

When she finally got home, it was starting to get dark. She had left her phone on the entry table, and she walked right past it into the kitchen. Hunger was making her stomach rumble but she didn't feel like cooking, so she rummaged around for a minute in the fridge and then abandoned it. Maybe she would go out again. Her phone was ringing from the hall, and she reluctantly went to see who it was. There were nights lately when she had forced herself to go out and socialize despite not feeling at all like it, but tonight was not going to be one of those nights.

It was Harper. They hadn't spoken again since their weird conversation a couple of weeks ago, though they did text one another occasionally. Lauren had been trying to settle into the idea that they just weren't going to be speaking much for a while, though she had never given up hope for them. She was considering offering to go out there in a couple of weeks for a visit and the thought excited her so much she felt a buzz every time it crossed her mind. The idea of seeing Harper again made her stomach flutter, but more importantly, she wanted to try to take the temperature of the situation. Now that they'd had some time apart, she would get a better idea of whether Harper might reconsider things.

"Hey!" she said when she answered. It was loud wherever Harper was, and at first she thought that Harper must have pocket-dialed her.

"Hey, what are you up to?" Harper said.

"Nothing much. Just deciding what to have for dinner. Where are you?"

Harper sounded happy. Maybe now was the right time to offer to visit her. "Sorry about the noise. So you're not with anyone or anything?"

"No, I'm alone," Lauren said.

"You should have pizza for dinner."

"I should?" Lauren replied. Harper was acting oddly. She wasn't sure how to ask delicately whether she was drunk.

"Yes, you still like pizza don't you? From Manny's?"

Definitely drunk, Lauren concluded. It was cute, but it also made her sad. Did Harper have to be drunk to make contact with her, to make a simple phone call to her? Lauren had to stop herself from quizzing Harper about whom she was with. There was no reason to be jealous when she was probably just out having a good time with friends, Lauren just wished that they were together.

"Yes, I still like pizza. What are you doing?"

"Just hanging out. I think you should go to Manny's."

"Okay, after I hang up I'll go to Manny's," Lauren said to placate her, though she had no intention of doing it. "Would that make you happy?"

"Yes it would," Harper said. "How soon can you get there?"

"Harper, what's up?"

"I'm really bad at this," Harper said.

"Bad at what? Are you okay?"

"Surprises. Can you just come to Manny's? I'm here," she said, laughter in her voice.

Lauren's eyes widened as she tried to process the information. "Are you serious?"

"Very. Now come join me, this is not the sort of place a lady should be sitting alone." Harper sounded like her usual jokey self, but Lauren could hear the nerves in her voice.

"Oh my god, you're really here?" Lauren said.

"I am."

Lauren thought she would cry with happiness. She felt foolish, worrying that she might never see Harper again. Of course Harper wouldn't let that happen. She must have been planning this visit the whole time.

"I can be there in twenty minutes. Don't go anywhere," Lauren said.

"Nowhere else I've got to be." The line went silent.

CHAPTER TWENTY-FOUR

It was the longest subway ride Lauren ever took. She ran down to the street, down the stairs, and onto the platform like a maniac. The wait for a train was only for a minute or two, but now she had to just sit. Part of her expected this all to be some sort of ridiculous prank, even though she knew Harper would never be that cruel. She couldn't wrap her mind around the idea that Harper was actually in the same city as she was.

Lauren planned to make the most of this visit. She had no idea how long Harper would be staying, but however long it was, Lauren wanted to use the time to convince her that somehow they could work this out. The fact that Harper was even here gave her immense hope. Harper wasn't the type to fly all the way to another state for a booty call or to casually catch up.

Lauren shifted in her seat impatiently. She wished she'd had time to change her clothes, but she hadn't wanted to delay seeing Harper for such a silly reason.

When she finally arrived, Lauren stood outside the bar for a moment to compose herself. It had been literally years since she had been here, although since she and Harper had talked about it, she'd considered dropping in over the last few weeks. Lauren pushed the door open and was met with the familiar sights and smells of the place. The sticky floors and the sound of clinking glasses brought with them a wave of nostalgia. A few people looked up as she came in, but only one face stayed turned to hers for more than a few seconds.

Lauren froze. She had become so accustomed to imagining Harper everywhere that the reality of actually seeing her was jarring. For a second she didn't quite trust her own perception. It was surreal, as though she had stepped into one of her own movies.

Harper nodded at her, but Lauren could see the grin threatening to break out on her face. Lauren threw her head back in the same nod and made her way over.

"Hey."

"Hey. I ordered us some pizza, it should be here soon."

"What kind?" Lauren said with narrowed eyes.

"Double pepperoni, of course."

"Good, that was a test," Lauren said.

"Did I pass?"

"Yep. You remembered my favorite," Lauren said. She slid her hand across the table and took Harper's hand. Her skin was warm and soft and unbelievably comforting. They stared at one another. Lauren wondered if she could ever get used to how beautiful Harper was.

"I'm sorry I didn't call more over the last month. I didn't want to tell you I was coming unless I was sure it was going to work out," Harper explained.

Lauren shrugged. She felt so giddy that she already couldn't remember how miserable and lonely she'd been. "It was worth it for the surprise. How long are you staying for?"

At that moment, the waiter arrived with the pizza and they stopped talking. Harper was watching Lauren's face.

"Where are you staying?" Lauren asked, looking around them to see if Harper had luggage with her. "I hope you haven't booked a hotel. You're staying at my place, of course?"

Harper raised an eyebrow at her. "You're a little fast, Ms. Langham. We've only been dating a while. It's far too soon for me to move in."

"Move in?" Lauren said, grinning. Harper was obviously as over the moon that they were together as she was, judging by the look on her face, but she wasn't making a lot of sense.

"I'll put you out of your misery. You remember me telling you about my uncle? I've gotten my old job back. I'm staying with him. I'm living here."

Lauren picked up a slice of pizza so she would have something to do with her shaking hands. The world had righted itself so suddenly that it made a lump rise in her throat. She had no idea how to react to the best piece of news she had ever heard in her life. Her happiness was too big for laughter or smiles, because she felt completely overcome.

Harper followed her lead and picked up a piece of pizza as well. "I hope you know I don't have big expectations of you or anything. There's no pressure. I was going to move here for work anyway."

"Try again, Harper."

"Try again?"

It was one of the first times Lauren could remember seeing Harper look fearful, so she smiled at her. "Yeah. Tell me again."

Harper nodded. She put down her pizza slice and grabbed both of Lauren's hands. "Lauren, I want to be with you. Do you still want that?"

"Sure, I guess," Lauren said, then laughed.

"Oh, you're horrible. You set me up," Harper replied.

"I did." They laughed, releasing the tension. Then Lauren leaned across and put her hand on the side of Harper's face. "I'm sorry. Yes, I do. Very much."

They ate quietly for a moment. Harper picked up another slice. Lauren watched with satisfaction as cheese stretched out and snapped off in a string. "I can't believe I can come here whenever I want. With you."

Lauren leaned her chin on her hand. "I feel like I've figured out a big secret."

"What type of secret?" Harper asked her.

"I don't know. The secret to happiness. That I don't need much to be happy. Just hanging out with you and having a good meal is more than enough for me."

"I know something else that would make me happy. Let's go back to your place," Harper said, wiping her greasy hands on a napkin and tossing it down on the table.

Lauren threw her head back and laughed. "You're right, what are we even still doing here?"

They linked arms and quickly made their way there, their feet barely touching the ground. While they went, Harper caught Lauren up on the relocation, explaining how her father had made it so much easier for her to go.

"I could get used to having a father-in-law like him," said Lauren. "We should go and visit him. I'd like to see him again."

"Well, he'll be even fonder of you when he finds out you're going to make sure I visit."

When they got to Lauren's apartment building, Lauren paused to talk to the doorman. "Eddie, this is Harper. You don't need to buzz me when she comes over, you can just let her right up."

"Pleased to meet you, ma'am," he said.

Lauren led her to the elevator and they stepped inside. Harper turned to her, and put her hands on Lauren's waist. "Alone at last."

Harper leaned forward and kissed her, feeling Lauren's fingers on her neck.

They broke apart and lay on their backs.

"I don't know how I went for so long without doing that," Harper said.

"Me neither," Lauren said, still catching her breath.

Harper rolled over and kissed Lauren's neck. "I like your place by the way. It's very you."

"I'm glad to hear it, especially because I'm planning on asking you to move in at an appropriate time. Or we can pick out a different place together. Whatever we want."

Harper smiled at her, nodding. "Let's see what's right when we get there."

Harper let herself into the apartment. It never ceased to thrill her just a little bit when Eddie or one of the other guys would wave her through, and then she'd slide her own key into the lock. Lauren had given it to her soon after she arrived in New York.

As she opened the door, she could smell that Lauren was cooking. She came over to Lauren's at least a few times a week for dinner, though they went out almost as often as they ate at home. Lauren had a million places that she wanted to introduce her to.

Lauren kept cheerfully saying that she was happily unemployed, though it wasn't quite accurate. There was one project in pre-production that she wasn't all that happy about because she had signed on before she had changed representation, but she was writing again. She had given Harper a couple of scripts to read and sought her opinion, to help her to decide on her next movie. From Harper's perspective, it seemed like things were going pretty well.

Harper slipped off her heels in the entry hall and pulled her blouse out from the waistband of her skirt. She rubbed her stocking-clad heel for a moment. She still wasn't used to having to dress in corporate attire for her job. There was little else to complain about, because she loved the work. It surprised her how quickly she had slipped back into it. Taking all that time off hadn't been great for her career, but she was starting to think that it would not be so long before it would be like it hadn't happened.

"Hey," she said. As usual, Lauren was listening to loud music and hadn't heard her come in.

"Oh, hey. My big important law lady, come here," Lauren said, and kissed her hello. Harper decided that maybe the clothes weren't so bad when they got that sort of reaction.

Harper took over stirring one of the pots on the stovetop when Lauren asked her to.

"Your dad called me just now," Lauren said. "I want to show you something."

Harper watched Lauren opened up a magazine. It looked like a glossy fashion rag, which was strange considering she had never seen her dad read anything that wasn't about cars or fishing.

"You're kidding. My dad called you about something in one of those magazines?"

"Well, he's dating isn't he? Maybe he saw one at a special friend's house," Lauren pointed out as she flipped through the pages. She held up the open magazine so Harper could see.

Harper gasped when she took in the fact that it was the two of them in the picture. It was fairly benign—they were just walking alongside one another on the street, but Lauren had an arm slung around her shoulder. It could be any morning, any day.

"Oh my God, how did they get that?"

"Long lenses," Lauren explained. "It's all over the Internet too, of course."

Harper turned off the hot plate so they could concentrate. She took the magazine from Lauren's hands and had a closer look at the article. "Lauren Langham Out and About with Gal Pal? Why is this news?"

"Saying 'gal pal' is them saying that they know we're probably together but they don't want to get sued," Lauren explained.

Harper put her hands over her mouth. "Oh wow, I see. Are you okay?"

Lauren put her arms around her. "I had a brief moment of freaking out, but I'm fine. I knew this might be coming. But you know what? Some people will get it and some people will never believe it for a second or just think we really are friends. Does it bother you? I know you didn't sign up for this. I hope it doesn't cause any problems at your work."

They hugged tightly and Harper scoffed. "I totally signed up for it. If it doesn't bother you then it doesn't bother me."

They finished cooking and took their bowls out into the living room. They often ate like this, stretched out on the floor with music playing and Chester running around them begging for scraps.

When they were like this, it was difficult for Lauren to remember how she could have felt any differently, how she could have ever been so frightened. With Harper at her side, backing her up, nothing felt threatening. Her heart was so open and free that it made all the stuff she used to worry about insignificant.

What the world thought of her didn't matter at all. The world was in this room, and it was full of only love.